CHESAPEAKE CRIMES 3

IN THE SAME SERIES

Chesapeake Crimes
Chesapeake Crimes 2

CHESAPEAKE CRIMES 3

Coordinating editors:

DONNA ANDREWS
AND MARCIA TALLEY

Editorial panel:

KAREN DIEGMUELLER
GAIL MEREDITH
MARY AUGUSTA THOMAS
LISA TILLMAN

WILDSIDE PRESS

CHESAPEAKE CRIMES 3

This is a work of fiction. All characters, organizations, places, and events portrayed in this collection of short stories are either products of the author's imagination or are used fictitiously.

This edition published in 2008 by Wildside Press, LLC.
www.wildsidebooks.com

CONTENTS

INTRODUCTION

Mild.

Who hasn't heard this left-handed compliment delivered to the loveliest section of the United States? Just because Maryland, D.C., Delaware, and Virginia rarely are lashed by hurricanes and buried in snow, the Chesapeake is inevitably labeled as milquetoast.

I cry foul, and not because I've been through more 100-degree Baltimore summers than I can remember, and have had my bathroom plumbing freeze every single winter as well. I'm talking foul play. The Chesapeake Bay area is home to strong winds, joys, and fears, where you lock your doors at night in the cities and probably should lock them too in the countryside, especially after reading this anthology.

Having had the pleasure of a sneak peek at the stories in this collection, I have found them as varied in tone and theme as the region itself. One of Maryland's favorite beaches, Cape Henlopen State Park, takes on a macabre twist in "Inked to Death" by Shelley Shearer, and the glamorous world of horse racing shows its ugly underside in "Pretty Fraudulent" by Sasscer Hill. The Eastern Shore casts its own inimitable shadow in Meriah Crawford's story, "It Tore the Laugh From My Throat," "The Tide Also Rises" by Jayne Ormerod, and "Crossing the Bridge" by Carolyn Mulford. The Bay Bridge proves deadly in quite unexpected ways in "Dangerous Crossing" by Carla Coupe, and the bay itself is a character in "Chimera" by Mary Ann Corrigan, "Troubled Waters" by Peggy Jaegley, and "The Serpeant's Tooth" by Mary Ellen Hughes. (A major pleasure is to read these water-stories and note that not a single character in these employs the stereotyped phrase *downy-ayshun* — because that's not how we all talk!)

In rural Virginia, though, good-old-boys still run wild; you'll find out if they get away with it in the stories "Compulsive Bubba" by Barb Goffman and "Backseat" by C. Ellett Logan. And within the region's two major cities, there are major troubles. You'll never think about open houses in upmarket Washington, D.C., the same way after experiencing

"The Lockbox" by G.M. Malliet, and you may become curious about a forgotten Baltimore neighborhood which forms the setting for "Two Sisters" by Marcia Talley. "Murder at Elk Neck" by K.B. Inglee, which takes a look at the key role the French provided in the War for Independence, is based on historical fact, as is the richly textured story of Jacksonian Washington, "Beede and the Barefoot Body," by Clyde Linsley.

The Chesapeake is a fascinating, checkerboard kind of place to live, and reading the stories in the collection gave me 15 reasons to wish I hadn't moved to the Midwest. I imagine that readers who've either lived in the Mid-Atlantic region or visit regularly may suffer pangs of homesickness when reading this book. And for the folks who are still living in this supposedly mild-mannered region, all I can say is, enjoy the weather, but watch your back.

—*Sujata Massey*

A Baltimore resident for 22 years, Sujata Massey was a features reporter at the now defunct Baltimore *Evening Sun*. She is also the author of ten mystery novels, one of which, *The Pearl Diver*, is set in Washington, D.C. Her Rei Shimura mysteries, which focus on the intersection of Japanese and American culture, have won the Agatha and Macavity awards and been nominated for the Edgar, Anthony, and Mary Higgins Clark awards. Currently she makes her home in Minneapolis with her husband, two children, and a Portuguese water dog.

CHIMERA

by Mary Ann Corrigan

Joe Hammersmith stood on his dock, calloused hands thrust in the pockets of his safari shorts. He'd left the construction site at noon, something he'd never done before. Work no longer mattered.

The Chesapeake sparkled, the sun reflected in its choppy surface like twinkling stars. Later, if the weather forecast held, the wind would pick up and the sky cloud over. A front would move in from the south, bringing scattered thunderstorms. A perfect day to die the way he wanted to, not hooked up to machines, not waiting in vain for a kidney donor.

He'd never thought of himself as the type to commit suicide. His survival instinct had kept him alive thirty-five years ago when the Vietcong had him surrounded. He'd eluded them and, after weeks alone in the jungle, located an American platoon. Now, with no hope of escaping his enemy, the disease weakening his resolve to live, he couldn't put a gun to his head and pull the trigger. Someone would find his body and see his brains splattered around, the way his buddy's brains had decorated the green foliage in 'Nam. No, Joe would rather exit the world intact. If he sailed to the middle of the bay and waited for the storm, he'd die doing what he loved. Not exactly suicide, but positioning himself for fate to take its course.

This exit would be easier on Chris. No fifteen-year-old wants to spend time with a dying man who isn't even his father. Of course, Chris had no idea Joe wasn't really his father. If Joe disappeared into the Chesapeake, would Mia tell the boy the truth? She'd denied it so convincingly when Joe confronted her, as if scientific proof meant nothing. Thought she could pull a fast one on her dumb husband who'd never gone to college. But Joe had excelled at biology and chemistry in high school. He subscribed to *Discover* magazine. He trusted science more than he trusted Mia. Maybe she believed in her own innocence because otherwise she couldn't live with herself.

She may have even grown to love him, but that love was rooted in a lie.

"Going out for a sail, Joe?"

He started at the sound of her voice and turned. "What are you doing home?"

Mia squinted in the sunlight, her eyes like the Chesapeake, sometimes blue, sometimes gray. "I called in sick this morning because Chris was still feeling bad. A substitute's covering my classes. I just got back from the supermarket."

Typical Mia, bending the rules. Until this year, Joe had never taken a sick day, even when he was sick. "Chris has a stomach bug. He doesn't need you hovering over him."

"You're right. He's feeling better already. So I can go out with you."

She couldn't resist the bay any more than he could. They loved sailing, one of the few things they had in common. The schoolteacher and the construction worker had found peace on the water, no matter how many disagreements they'd had on land. Did she think that sailing together would make him forget her betrayal?

"I'd rather sail alone," he muttered.

Mia, already half-way across the weedy lawn to the clap-board house, gave no sign she'd heard him. "I'll get my wind-breaker and tell Chris we're going," she said over her shoulder.

From the rear, she looked like a teenager, slight of frame, her hair in a ponytail. Maybe the twelve-year gap in their ages had been the root of their problems. He imagined her at his funeral, a fetching widow in her forties, bait for all the divorced men in Dorchester County. The thought sickened him.

She was responsible for his death sentence. If she hadn't betrayed him, he might now have a son of his own whose kidney could save him. Instead, she'd carried someone else's child and had so many complications that doctors warned against another pregnancy.

Now she was intruding on his perfect day, ruining his plans. Or maybe not. If a storm came up, he'd sit on his hands, let her sail the sloop. She'd have trouble getting to shore without his help. She, too, might have the perfect death.

Mia came back to the dock with Chris. The boy moved with his usual athletic grace, though his face looked pasty from his bout with a virus. A recent growth spurt had made him as tall as Joe. He would turn into a fine man. Joe's rage at Mia did not extend to the boy. He ached at the thought of not living long enough to see Chris reach manhood.

Joe smiled at him. "Gonna see us off?"

"Nah. I feel better. I want to go along, get some fresh air."

Joe sighed. With the boy aboard, he really couldn't go through with the plan.

He navigated toward the broadest expanse of the bay. As he expected, few boaters had come out on this weekday in mid-April. How Joe hated to lose this opportunity.

Then the wind picked up, and so did Joe's luck. Chris felt sick and descended into the cabin to lie down. Joe sailed tight to the wind, making for a rough ride. The boy wouldn't emerge from the cabin any time soon.

Mia pointed to the southwestern sky. "Weather's turning."

"It'll hold off." Joe stayed his course, aiming for the middle of the bay, equidistant from the Maryland and Virginia shores.

Mia glanced alternately at the sky and at him, her forehead furrowed, her mouth pursed. "What's wrong with you, Joe? Are you still brooding about that DNA nonsense? How could you possibly think Chris isn't your son?" She sounded patient, as if trying to talk sense into an unruly adolescent.

"He don't look like me."

"He does so. You don't see what's in front of your face. I've put up with your jealousy for sixteen years. Every time a man so much as glanced at me, your imagination ran away with you."

"Just say you're sorry. That's all I'm asking."

"I have nothing to be sorry for." She spoke through clenched teeth. "Chris *is* your son. They must have labeled those blood samples wrong."

"They did two tests, two different labs. They're both wrong?"

"Yes! I swear to God, there was no one else but you — ever." Her eyes pleaded with him. After a minute, she stood up. "I'll go down and check on Chris."

"Aw, leave 'im alone. Don't fuss over him."

She disappeared down the companionway and came up a few minutes later, her windbreaker zipped, its hood over her head. Joe barely glanced at his wife. Controlling the sloop in the gusts and choppy waters took all his concentration.

"Turn back. It's getting rough." She shouted over the wind, her usually low voice now high and impatient. "Chris will be sick all over the cabin."

Vomit in the cabin. Maybe that would have annoyed him a few weeks ago, but not anymore. He took a deep breath. "I'll take down the sails. We'll motor back." He steered into the wind.

"Can I help?"

"I'm having trouble with the jib halyard. See what's going on up there."

She climbed on top of the cabin and crawled toward the bow. She hadn't bothered to put on a tether and clip it to the lifelines.

Joe made his move. Wind hit the sail, and the boat tipped sideways. She lost her balance and clung to the lifeline.

Joe sprang toward her. "We're both going over. You first."

Her eyes widened. "Don't, Joe. Think about Chris."

"Before I jump, I'll call him up to the deck. He'll make it to shore."

"No!" she wailed.

He shoved her overboard. She hit the water with a splash, bobbed up, and yelled for Chris.

She'd put a life jacket on under her windbreaker, hadn't trusted Joe to sail back to shore. The jacket wouldn't save her. She'd die of hypothermia instead of drowning.

Chris burst from the cabin. "Mom!" He dove into the water. He, too, wore a life jacket. Mia must have gotten him to put it on when she went below.

"Chris!" Joe bellowed. "Stay near the boat."

The boy swam toward his mother and away from the boat. A brave boy. He deserved to live.

Joe punched the Man Overboard button on the GPS

plotter so the Coast Guard could find them, released the sheets to drop the sails, and started the engine.

He motored toward the spot where he'd last sighted two heads above the water. No Mia. No Chris. They must be in the troughs of the waves where he couldn't see them. The rain grew heavier and reduced visibility to a few yards. He kept searching.

A wave came over the stern, filling the cockpit and cabin.

The icy water shocked Joe. He clung to the sinking boat. This is what he'd wanted, right? Burial at sea. Just let go.

He couldn't. Maybe a miracle current would carry Chris and Mia toward him. The three of them would hang on until the Coast Guard rescued them.

Joe's hopes sank along with the boat. His legs pumped and his arms moved, anything to stay above water. Why was it so hard to die?

Scenes from the last few weeks came back to him. The grim diagnosis of his kidney disease. The slim hope Dr. Banjeri offered of finding an organ donor. The love that overwhelmed Joe when Chris offered a kidney to save his father. The shock of finding out that Chris, tested as a possible kidney donor, had DNA that didn't match Joe's. His fury at Mia for having an affair and foisting someone else's son on him.

He gave himself up to the water. Just when he thought he was going down for the last time, something tugged at him, pulled him up, and held his head above water. Then he was lying on a deck, puking the bay water he'd taken in, his throat raw. Saved by the Coast Guard. Saved, for what?

Between retches, he asked about Mia and Chris. "My wife and son? Did anyone pick them up?"

"Not yet."

He asked again and again. "Not yet" gave way to "No." They whispered of hypothermia.

The next few hours passed in a blur. A sheriff's deputy and an emergency medical team met the Coast Guard boat when it docked. Though his vital signs checked out, the EMTs urged him to go to the Emergency Room. He refused.

The deputy drove him to a substation to file a report. He

told them a swell had knocked his wife and son overboard, and stuck to that story. Though guilt oppressed him, he wouldn't confess his crime. Spend his final days on earth in a jail? Never. He couldn't tell if the deputies believed him, but they seemed sympathetic to his grief. They drove him home.

He sat on the sofa in shock. The phone rang. News of Mia and Chris? He picked it up.

Joe heard the familiar clipped tones of his Indian-born kidney specialist.

"Dr. Banjeri here. I have wonderful news for you."

Joe snorted. Dr. Banjeri had never given him any good news. Then he felt a pang, an icicle in his heart. "Those DNA tests? Were they wrong?"

"Oh, no! Certainly not. We did them twice, you know. The news is that you, Mr. Hammersmith, are a most unusual specimen — a chimera."

"A what? How do you spell that?"

Joe jotted the word on the pad next to the phone and asked the doctor to hold the line. He reached for the dictionary. He always had it handy because Mia had flaunted her education, using words he didn't understand.

> Chimera: *(1) a fire-breathing monster in myth. (2) an illusion or grotesque figment of imagination. (3) an individual or organ, consisting of tissues of diverse genetic constitution.*

The third definition sounded medical. Joe had no idea what it meant.

He picked up the phone. "So, Dr. Banjeri, are you saying I have a — uh — diverse genetic constitution?"

"Exactly so, Mr. Hammersmith. Here is the great good news. With two genetic strains, you have a much better chance of finding a suitable donor kidney."

"I don't want a kidney anymore." He had nothing to live for and didn't deserve spare parts. "How did I get to be a — a chimera?"

"This is a rare situation, less so in recent years because of fertilization in Petri dishes. But we can assume at your age you were not fertilized outside the womb. There was another little

Hammersmith in the womb with you, a fraternal twin, but just for a short time, until your embryo swallowed his embryo."

Sadness washed over Joe. He would have liked having a brother. "How do you know this, Doctor?"

"The last time you were here, I took a new blood sample, which is what we use for tissue typing, but also I swabbed your cheek, pulled a hair from your head, and got — uh — other fluids, if you recall."

As if he could forget taking a *Hustler* magazine into that little room and jacking off on demand for the doctor. "Yes and . . ."

"Some of your systems have your original DNA, some have the DNA from your twin. Your blood carries one type, and your saliva, skin, and semen have another strain. When I reported that your lad's DNA didn't match yours, I could see the agony in your face. Any man would be shocked to discover his children were not his own. But now, I can set your mind to rest. The lad is indeed your son. Isn't that grand news? What's more —"

Joe dropped the phone, his eyes on the open dictionary. There he saw the truth about himself. A single word with three meanings summed up his life. Born a biological chimera, obsessed with the chimera of his wife's guilt, raging with the fire of jealousy, he had morphed into a monster.

Mary Ann Corrigan, an instructional designer, has taught writing, detective fiction, and drama at Georgetown University and other colleges, and contributed nonfiction to five anthologies. She lives in Virginia, a short drive from Maryland's Eastern Shore, the setting for her story and the tennis mystery series she hopes to have published. The initial book in the series, *The Murder Racquet*, was a finalist in the 2008 St. Martin's Press Malice Domestic Competition. Her boating memories — of squalls, seasickness, and capsizing — prompted her to set her story aboard a small vessel in a storm.

DANGEROUS CROSSING

by Carla Coupe

I hit the wall of fog as I passed the outlet mall on Route 50. The mist engulfed my car, muffling sound, even with the windows open. Like walking into a greenhouse in the dead of winter, the saturated air relaxed my tight skin, moisture collected on my hair. I took a deep breath and turned on my headlights. My red Prius caught attention, but with fog this thick I didn't want to take the chance of being overlooked, especially by all the trucks out at this hour of the morning.

I wasn't risk averse or anything. I liked rock climbing and sailing, and bungee jumped once. I'd spent this warm early May weekend bike riding and walking along the shore, being as active as possible, in contrast to the sedentary desk job that paid my rent. I'd also stopped by the arcade once. Or twice. Okay, three times, but only because I wanted to play the ring toss again and win the big stuffed dog for my nephew.

Following the big, lazy curve that joined Route 50 with 301, I figured it would take just over an hour to get home to Bethesda. I settled into the middle lane, passing a convoy of lumbering dump trucks and being passed in turn by a couple of long-haul semis and a young blonde in a yellow Mustang.

I glanced in my rear-view mirror. A black Charger roared out of the vacant whiteness, slipped into the left lane behind one of the semis, and pulled up beside me. The car swerved without warning, almost hitting me. I honked and jerked the wheel, ending up half-way into the — thankfully empty — right lane. What the hell?

The Charger pulled ahead. I glared at the car, full of broad shoulders and beefy necks, and decided not to flip them the bird. I was angry, not stupid.

The semi in front slowed, forcing the Charger back beside me. The shoulders and necks shifted position. A hand pressed flat against the rear passenger window, then disappeared. Weird.

My cell phone rang — Big Ben's chimes — eerily appropriate in the fog. My best friend Margy, an ardent Anglophile, had programmed my new phone and selected her ring tone. Easy for a technical wizard, but I had trouble answering the thing without disconnecting.

I retrieved my phone from the front pocket of my small backpack, which I used instead of a purse while traveling. I flipped the phone open and held it to my left ear as a flash lit the side of the car. Great. I'd pressed the camera button by mistake. Again.

A horn sounded as the Charger sped past me. Damned aggressive drivers.

"So, Trish, have you met Mr. Right?" Margy's admitted goal was to find me a man as fine as her husband. I wasn't holding my breath.

"Well, there was Chip, a doctor I met at Dogfish Head." The Charger pulled in front of me and slowed. I braked sharply and bit back a curse.

"A doctor! How old?"

"Early forties." The Charger accelerated again and I hit the gas.

"Good. Not too young, but not too old. What did you talk about?"

"How much he misses his wife since their separation."

In front of me, the Charger's brake lights lit up again. I stomped on the brake pedal and clutched the wheel one-handed. The road was clear ahead, damn him. Could he be pissed off because I'd honked at him earlier? Wasn't he the one driving recklessly?

"Margy, traffic's a bear." A muted siren sounded. The fog made it hard to pinpoint its direction. "I'll call back when I get home." Flipping my phone closed, I tried to tuck it back into its pocket in my backpack, but fumbled as the Charger veered into the right lane. Damn it! My phone fell to the floor and slid under the seat.

The Charger disappeared into the fog at the next exit.

A police car, siren screaming, lights flashing, rushed by, sending eddies and swirls of fog whipping across the pavement in its wake.

I drove over the graceful arch of the Kent Narrows Bridge but couldn't see a hint of Prospect Bay — beautiful on a clear day, wooded inlets dotted with houses. The view from the Bay Bridge, stretching over four miles across the Chesapeake, would be even more spectacular. Cars traveled along decking suspended high above the water, and from that vantage even huge container ships looked small. In fog this thick, however, I'd be lucky to see the second span a couple hundred feet away.

Another police car passed me, flashing lights reflecting on the fog like those in a rock concert.

An accident ahead? As I passed Romancoke Road — the last exit before the bridge — I checked the overhead lane signs. A red X blazed over the left lane. Just my rotten luck. The northern span, usually three lanes traveling west, now designated the far left lane for cars traveling east. I hated the two-way traffic pattern; it was unnerving when cars headed toward you on a bridge with no shoulder. I pulled into the far right lane and heard waves crashing over the breakwater on either side of the road as I drove onto the bridge.

Up the gentle curve of the span, concrete joints thunk-thunking under my tires, I passed under the lattice of steel beams that supported the bridge decking. A pickup overloaded with bricks and bags of cement crawled in the right lane, forcing me over into the middle. The oncoming stream of cars broke free of the fog, lights blurry in the mist, hurrying by on my left. The acrid breeze stirred by their passing brushed my cheeks and dampened my hair, but I didn't want to close the window.

A horn blared. I jumped in my seat and almost steered into the oncoming traffic. The Charger rode my rear bumper, honking wildly. Where the hell did he come from? I'd seen him exit the highway. An enormous moving van occupied the right lane, leaving me nowhere to go. Desperate to let the Charger pass, I sped up as much as I dared. Despite the chilly air, I was sweating, and had to release my death-grip on the steering wheel to wipe my clammy hands, one at a time, on my jeans.

As soon as I could, I moved into the right lane, but the Charger stayed on my tail, nearly cutting off the moving van. What was he doing? Didn't he want to pass? I slowed down, but he bumped me from behind, a quick jolt that made my teeth rattle.

Oh, my God. He wanted me to stop.

Was he crazy? Why was he picking on me?

No way was I going to stop my car. Not on the bridge, and not just me facing a car full of big guys. I needed help. I'd cross the bridge and stop at the Transportation Authority building on the other side, where at least I could find a policeman and some shelter.

The Charger bumped me again. I stepped on the gas and cut back into the middle lane, right in front of a tan Suburban. When the Charger tried to follow, horns blared. He'd almost hit the Suburban and had to swing back into the right lane. It looked as if the driver realized his Charger wouldn't win that battle and backed off.

I couldn't believe what was happening. Like something out of a bad horror movie — innocent heroine chased by. . . who? Who were these guys?

I had a minute or two to catch my breath as I traveled over the span's midpoint, then the Suburban moved into the right lane. My stomach twisted as I saw the Charger's headlights reflect in my mirror, and I pressed the accelerator. Dangerous to speed in that fog, but even more dangerous to let him catch me.

A row of cars and trucks lined the right lane, preventing me from moving over. I kept my foot to the floor. He wove from side to side, then bumped me again. I clutched the wheel, trying to stay in my lane. Suddenly, during a break in the oncoming traffic, the Charger darted into the far left lane — God, he'd kill me or some innocent traveler — and blindly raced ahead. A white box truck broke from the fog heading straight for the Charger, horn blasting. I stomped on my brakes. The Charger careened past my hood at the last second, but he overcompensated, sliding into the right lane, glancing off the side of a UPS van.

The van hit the bridge rail, then bounced back and hit the Charger again. On the other side, the box truck clipped my rear fender, then skidded across two lanes and plowed into the Suburban, metal screeching.

The Charger spun around as the UPS van scraped two cars, then hit an oncoming tractor trailer, forcing it to swerve across traffic, tilting precariously. Arrhythmic bass thunks rattled the span as cars and trucks banged together, accompanied by the treble of smashing glass and buckling metal. Earsplitting. It sounded like some bizarre demolition punk concert.

My head spun, but I managed to stop before I hit the semi, which now lay on its side, stretched across the bridge from railing to railing. Another sedan nudged me on the passenger side, pushing me toward the trailer. Time to get the hell out of Dodge, before someone else accordioned me into the semi, or ripped open my gas tank, sending the car — and me — up in a fireball.

No time to look for my phone, still somewhere under the seat. Reports from dozens of witnesses probably clogged the emergency lines already. I grabbed my backpack, which held my wallet and toiletries, and scrambled out of my poor car, shaking so hard I had trouble walking. Over on the right — how had he ended up there? — the Charger faced backward, driver's side resting against the railing. Blood coated the inside of the shattered windshield. I took an involuntary step toward the car. The door opened, and a burly guy with black hair in a crew cut rolled out, followed by another guy, just as big, with a shaved head and mirrored aviator sunglasses. Sunglasses in fog? They looked as dazed as I felt. Were the guys still in the car injured? Or dead?

The two big guys didn't seem to care. They took a couple staggering steps, looking around. Baldy spotted me and pointed. "There's the bitch!"

Crewcut looked at me and smiled.

The chill in my belly turned to ice. I felt like a bug about to have its wings pulled off. No humor, no humanity, just cruel enjoyment in that smile. No doubt if he caught me, he'd kill me.

Why? What had I done to them? They were the ones who'd almost caused an accident earlier, who'd hounded me and caused all this carnage. Road rage on crystal meth. It still didn't explain why he looked at me with cold, snake eyes.

A knot of people had gathered to my right, banging on a car door, trying to get someone out. They were farther away than Baldy and Crewcut, though, and on the other side of the mass of crumpled metal that blocked the entire width of the bridge. If I could somehow make it over to them. . . .

Before I could take a step, the bridge rocked as a car exploded between me and the crowd. A woman screamed. People scattered and I ducked behind my Prius, burning debris landing on the pavement — confetti from hell.

I peered over the top of the car. Baldy leaned inside the Charger, while Crewcut had moved closer. He and the burning car cut me off from the others.

"Help!" My scream blended with other cries, the sounds falling dead in the saturated air. No one even looked my way.

Baldy backed from the car, a dark shape in his hand. He tucked it into the waistband of his jeans, then made his way over to Crewcut.

A gun. He had a gun. Would he be stupid and blatant enough to try to kill me here, in front of witnesses?

The way the Charger had threatened me on the road, I wouldn't put anything past him.

Face the facts; I didn't have many choices. Keep out of sight, and find something to defend myself with if they got too close. Plenty of crumpled metal and burning debris, but nothing resembling a weapon. My hooded raincoat, tee-shirt, and jeans wouldn't be any help. I checked my car. In the door pocket of my Prius I kept an orange escape hammer — the kind you could use to smash a window or cut a seatbelt if you were trapped. My dad had bought it for me for my birthday, along with a roadside emergency kit and a gallon of windshield washer fluid. I hefted it: heavy, with a wicked metal point.

If I got out of this alive, I'd never complain about my dad's choice of gifts again.

Slipping on my backpack and keeping low, I crept toward the left side of the bridge, away from Baldy and Crewcut. I needed to get around the truck; the police were probably already there, and I'd have a straight shot down the bridge to safety. Maybe I could scoot along the outside of the rail. . . .

My heart sank as I neared the truck's tail. The back of the truck had crushed the rail, projecting crumpled metal a foot over the edge of the deck. No way around for me unless I had a rope and no fear of heights. No to both of those.

To my left stood a huge concrete pier that anchored the suspension cables holding up the roadbed. The gently curved top measured about ten feet square. If the truck had landed a yard or two closer, I could have climbed out onto the concrete mesa and walked around the truck.

No chance of that.

Two curved pieces of metal at the edge of the pier caught my eye. A ladder?

I glanced back. Baldy and Crewcut rounded my Prius and sauntered toward me, as if they had all the time in the world. They thought they had me cornered.

I stuck the hammer in my raincoat pocket and scrambled onto the pier, heading for the ladder. It probably led to a catwalk or platform of some sort, maybe even a way around the wrecked semi. Good thing I had my running shoes on — the fog made everything slick.

"Hey! Where's she going?"

Baldy's voice. A laugh that sounded like the trickle of ice water made my stomach lurch.

"Don't matter. She won't get far."

I probably wouldn't. From what little I knew of the matter, thrillseekers were usually prevented from getting access to service areas by a locked gate or some sort of barrier.

I reached the ladder. My feet and hands slipped on the handrails and rungs, but I didn't have time to be careful. A rudimentary cage around the ladder prevented me from falling to my death as I half-climbed, half-slid twenty feet down to a wire mesh platform. Fog floated thickly under the little platform, cutting off my view down to the water. A long way down.

The platform, open on the left, led to a mesh catwalk suspended under the bridge. The fog whited out the walk a dozen feet farther. My biggest problem was the chain link gate between me and the catwalk. I tried turning the handle. Locked.

The gate sat flush with the concrete and girders on my right, and overshot the railing by around a foot on my left. If I could climb the rail and swing around the protruding flange of the gate — ignoring the drop below — I could get onto the catwalk.

My fingers slipped on the damp wire mesh. I climbed up onto the rail, clinging to the chain link gate.

"I'll get her." I froze at the sound of Crewcut's voice rolling down the ladder. "You keep watch," he continued.

"You want the gun?"

"Nah. Don't let anyone down here. Maybe I'll have a little fun with the bitch first." A promise in his tone belied the spoken 'maybe.' The metal rungs creaked.

My hands shook, my stomach knotted. I had to get to the other side.

I swung my leg around the gate, rested my foot on the far railing, and inched along, pretending there was a floor right under the fog, only five or six feet down. Not a hundred.

The gate rattled as I shifted my weight from one side to the other. Booted feet appeared on the ladder. I forced my arms and legs to move faster, trying not to pause over the drop.

I scrambled off the rail on the far side of the gate as Crewcut reached the platform and turned. His look of surprise — he probably expected me to be cowering in a corner — was gratifying for a second, then he scowled.

"Give me the camera."

I backed away a step, confused. "Camera? I don't have —"

"Bullshit! I saw the flash!" He unclenched his fists and rolled his shoulders. His chest was a wall of muscle.

The flash. My phone. Was that what all this was about? Because I'd taken a picture of their car?

"My phone." I hated the quiver in my voice. "A mistake. I didn't mean to. . ."

"So give me your phone." His scowl deepened and he took a step forward.

"It fell in the car. Under the seat."

"If you're lying. . ." A hard stare, then he turned, one booted foot slipping on the wet mesh flooring, and returned to the ladder. "Franks!" He called up the shaft.

I pulled off my backpack. Crewcut would come after me. I only had a few seconds to try to stop him or slow him down. I found what I was looking for and set to work.

"Check in her car, under the seat. A phone." Crewcut

paused, as if listening. "Don't think she saw anything, but I'll take care of her, just in case."

I dropped the little tube of hand lotion into my backpack and stepped back, wiping my greasy hands on my jeans.

He grinned as he approached the gate. Rubbed his crotch, making sure I could see the bulge. "Oh yeah, I'll take care of you."

"Why?" I swallowed hard, fingered the hammer in my pocket. "What did I take a picture of?"

"None of your business." He looked over the gate, decided to climb around, as I had done.

Good.

"I didn't see anything." My voice rose. "Take my phone. Just leave me alone."

He didn't answer. Crewcut hooked his fingers in the chain link of the gate and climbed onto the rail.

I waited, watching, as he reached one hand around to the other side of the gate, then shifted his weight and swung his leg around, setting his booted foot onto the rail.

His foot slipped on the hand lotion I'd spread over the railings. He yelled once, and I darted forward. Crewcut struggled to keep his awkward hold on the chain link — one hand on either side of the gate, the metal frame cutting into his chest — his legs flailing over the drop as he tried to find purchase on the lotion-slick rail.

Hammer ready, I swung at his hand, catching him across his knuckles. He screamed and cursed as I hit his hand over and over, trying not to think about what I was doing. I had to break his hold, stop him from getting around the gate, or I'd be the one dead.

His battered hand slipped first, then the other. He grunted, fingers scrabbling for purchase. With a last snarl, he fell, disappearing into the fog. I didn't hear a splash.

My hands shook, my knees gave way. I collapsed onto the catwalk.

I stared at the hammer, evidence of what I'd done. And what I had yet to do. Slick with blood and sweat, it slipped from my numb fingers and bounced over the edge of the walkway, swallowed by the fog that had taken Crewcut.

No. My only weapon, gone. I wanted to cry, or puke. Or both. I was screwed.

"Hey, Tyler!" The voice sounded flat, as if it wanted to echo down the ladder, but the fog deadened the sound. "Can't find her fucking phone — she must be lying."

Baldy. And he had a gun.

"Tyler?"

He didn't have to climb around the gate; he could shoot me from the other side.

I had to move if I had any hope of surviving. I scrambled to my feet, grabbed my backpack and ran three yards to the main catwalk that hung directly below the center of the bridge deck. The gate vanished behind me as I took a left and started down the length of the bridge. My footsteps thudded on the mesh flooring.

Somehow I had to get past him, get back onto the bridge deck proper, where there were people, the police.

I ran down the catwalk. Maybe there was another ladder, and I could climb up further along the bridge. I couldn't see more than ten feet ahead or behind, as if I were cocooned in a cloud, invisible. About eight feet above the catwalk ran another stretch of mesh grid, probably to protect the catwalk from debris falling from the roadbed. A yell behind me. Baldy — Franks — had made it down the ladder.

He'd be after me.

I tried to be quiet, but the catwalk vibrated with every step. Once I stopped, listening. I could feel Franks's footsteps. My mouth went dry, and I took off again.

Almost ran headlong into another concrete pier. The catwalk ended in a T junction at the pier, branching to the left and right. I ran down the one to the left: nothing. No ladder, no way up to the decking. Only a chain link barrier at the far end of the catwalk.

Please, I prayed, let there be a ladder on the other side. I almost screamed with frustration and fright when I saw that the same chain link fence hemmed me in on that side, as well.

I sobbed once; I didn't have time to break down. Not if I wanted out of this alive.

My backpack landed with a thud on the catwalk. I slipped

off my raincoat. Rummaging in my backpack, I pulled out my wallet and a container of dental floss and shoved them into my back pockets. I might not have the chance to retrieve the pack later.

With my raincoat and backpack in hand, I ran back until I could barely see the junction with the main catwalk. I placed the backpack at the edge of the catwalk and draped my raincoat over the pack, letting the material fall over the side, under the lowest rail. With the hood up and the arms pulled forward, I hoped that in the fog it would appear as if I was climbing over the edge of the catwalk.

In the distance, I heard Franks still yelling for Tyler. I stopped halfway between the junction and my decoy. Kneeling, I tied one end of the dental floss to the lower rail, then stretched it across the catwalk. My hands shook as I wrapped the floss around the rail and brought it back, trying to keep it as tight as possible. It took me three tries to tie it off. Franks's voice made my fingers clumsy. Done, at last.

I inched across the junction, trying not to make the catwalk vibrate more than necessary. I couldn't breathe — the fog smothered me, caught in my lungs and throat, made me wheeze. I clapped my hand over my mouth. Franks mustn't hear me.

I backed up until I couldn't see the junction, just soft swirls of mist.

"Tyler! God damn it, answer me!"

I crouched, making myself as inconspicuous as possible. Ready to move.

The catwalk shook with his heavy steps, rattled my bones, set my teeth chattering.

"You bitch, where did you. . ."

He stopped, then laughed, soft and low. Cold trickled down my spine. "Trying to climb down, are you?" The catwalk shook as he ran toward the decoy. "Think you can get away —"

A crash and clatter. He'd tripped on the floss and hit the mesh flooring. He yelled — "God damn it, my gun!"

I ran.

I rounded the corner at the junction and glanced at Franks

as he lay on the deck. When I pounded down the catwalk, I could hear him behind me.

Gaining on me.

I hoped the gun had gone over the edge of the deck, but it didn't matter now. I had to get to the gate, climb around it and up the ladder before he caught me.

Or else.

He didn't waste his breath shouting at me — the clang of our footsteps rang in my ears. Keep going, don't slip, faster, faster, faster. . .

A grunt behind me echoed my own as I fell heavily onto the catwalk — he'd tackled me. I screamed and tried to scramble to my feet, but he wrapped his arms around my waist, cutting off my breath. Kicking, scratching, jabbing with my heels and elbows — I'd bite if anything came within range — I had to get him off me.

He held on, panting curses and hot air onto my back, dragging me upright as he staggered to his feet. Almost a foot taller than me and at least fifty pounds of solid muscle heavier, he lifted me off my feet, swinging me toward the rail.

Ready to drop me over the edge.

I braced my feet on the rail — for a heart-stopping moment one shoe slipped — then I gained my footing and pushed hard, shoving him back to the other side of the catwalk. He landed against the far railing with a grunt. For a second his grip loosened and I desperately tried to break free, but he recovered, squeezing me even tighter, lifting me higher.

Reaching up, I grabbed the mesh grid suspended over the catwalk. Not much leverage, but it gave me some stability, enough to twist around, kick him in the gut. He loosened his grip and I lifted my knee, slamming it against his chin. His head jerked back and he released me, raised his hands to his bloodied face with a howl.

I hung by my hands, rough wire mesh cutting into my fingers. Kicking and flailing, frantic to keep him off-balance, I focused on his face, his belly, and below. He turned away to protect himself, bent over the railing as I kicked his spine and tailbone, my legs growing heavy, my hands and arms aching.

I let go, crashing to the catwalk in a heap. I don't know how

I did it, but I managed to grab his calves before he could turn. I lifted him, fear fueling my strength, the rail cutting into his lower belly acting as a fulcrum — the downside of being so tall.

Hanging over the outside of the rails, he grabbed the bottom rail as I shoved his legs higher, trying to keep him from kicking me. Strong, he packed a punch like a mule as I struggled to keep my arms wrapped around his calves.

I lifted him enough that the rail bit into his thighs, his center of gravity tipping to the outside. Then I let go, caught his feet, pushed them over.

He must've realized I'd succeed in tipping him over the rail because he'd twisted, shifted his grip so he now hung on the outside, facing the catwalk. He clung to the rail and stared at me. He'd lost his mirrored shades, his dark eyes burned. My body shook, trembling with fear and exhaustion, and I slumped against the far rail, watching him.

I should have kicked his hands, loosened his grasp, but I couldn't. I'd sent one man to his death already. Yes, I'd had to do it or he would've killed me. That didn't change the fact of what I had done, didn't make it any easier to bear.

We stared at each other, tears blurring my vision. He groaned and swung his legs, trying to hoist them onto the catwalk, but he couldn't lift them high enough — he was tiring. The fingers on his left hand slipped, and for a long moment he hung, suspended by one hand. With a grunt, he grabbed for the rail, missed, and grabbed again.

His right hand slipped.

He tried to catch hold of the catwalk but couldn't. I watched him fall into the mist and disappear.

Three tries before I staggered to my feet, exhausted body and soul. I scrubbed the tears from my cheeks before I made my way back down the catwalk to retrieve my backpack and raincoat. He'd broken the dental floss when he fell. I unwrapped it from the rail, tossed it away, then slogged back to the gate.

Safe. I couldn't believe it. I only had to get to the other side of the gate.

I climbed the chain link gate, unwilling to become an ironic anecdote or finalist in the Darwin Awards: the woman who had escaped death twice only to fall from a bridge from sheer carelessness.

Sweating and almost limp from exhaustion, I made it to the other side of the gate. Just the climb up the ladder, and I'd be able to tell my wild tale to the police.

Wild tale, indeed. I'd better find my phone before I said anything, check out the photo I'd taken. I'd need all the evidence I could get to prove my side of the story.

The clamor grew as I climbed — the wail of sirens, shouting voices, the occasional scream of rending metal — and I dragged myself onto the top of the pier, greeted by chaos.

Uniformed police officers, firemen, and emergency medical technicians clustered around cars, tending to the injured, or cataloguing the dead. They'd doused the car fire that had cut me off. The area around my car and the Charger was deserted — either they'd come and gone or hadn't reached it yet.

Franks had searched my car, pulling up the carpet and almost ripping the seats from their frames. He hadn't found my phone, but he had big arms and hands. Maybe it had slipped completely under the seat and he couldn't reach it.

I squeezed into the back seat, lay down, and reached under the front passenger seat, fingers blindly searching.

My hand brushed over a smooth surface. Found it.

As I scrambled out of my car, a uniformed officer walked over to the Charger and peered inside. He leaned forward, then climbed half-way into the car. I walked over to him, waiting until he was finished. No hurry. Not now.

"Hey!" The policeman yelled as he backed out. "Over here!" He gestured to a pair of EMTs standing beside the UPS van. "We have an injured officer!"

The officer ran to another car before I could speak, while the EMTs did what they could with their patient in situ, then started to extract him from the car. I overheard one EMT report that the driver was dead, but the injured policeman had a good chance of surviving. I had to be patient, wait until one of the busy officers had time to listen to me. While I waited, I decided to try to view the photo I'd taken. It might contain evidence that explained why Tyler and Franks wanted me dead.

I needed a couple of attempts before successfully navigating the menu, but I managed to display the photo at last.

I gulped. No wonder Franks and Tyler were worried. The picture was blurred, still I could see Tyler sitting in the front passenger seat, holding the arms of a guy in the middle of the backseat. Franks sat behind Tyler, one hand in the other guy's long blond hair, pulling back his head. The guy on the far side — I couldn't see his face, but curly gray hair haloed his head — held a knife to the blond guy's throat.

I closed my eyes. The image burned at the back of my eyelids.

Maybe they hadn't cut the blond guy's throat after all? Or had he just been injured, and survived both his injury and the accident?

Maybe my camera flash had stopped them, saving Blondie's life, and he'd been knocked out by the crash?

"Excuse me, miss." Someone jostled me and I opened my eyes. I stepped back and had a clear view of the injured policeman on the stretcher.

I stared at the man, my gut twisting. I didn't care that bruises and gashes covered his face or about his bloody hands and clothes. All I could see was the curly gray hair that surrounded his head.

A police officer. The man with the knife was a policeman.

Had Franks and Tyler been policemen, too? I glanced into the Charger; only the driver's broken corpse still there. They must have dumped the blond man's body before coming after me.

I stared at the picture on my phone.

"Miss? Are you okay?"

I looked up. The uniformed officer frowned.

"Are you injured?"

I shook my head.

"Which car is yours?"

"The Prius." My tongue felt too large for my mouth.

He looked around at the carnage. "Can you tell me what happened?"

I glanced at the Charger, my eyes passing over the twisted wrecks of car and trucks, skimming over the concrete pier and ladder, only to end up staring at the photo on my phone.

I swallowed hard and flipped the phone shut.

"I don't know how it started, officer. It must've been the fog."

Carla Coupe stays busy as secretary of the Mid-Atlantic Chapter of Mystery Writers of America and an active member of Sisters in Crime. Her Agatha Award-nominated short story, "Rear View Murder," appeared in *Chesapeake Crimes 2*. When she isn't writing, you can find her in her garden or belly dancing.

IT TORE THE LAUGH FROM MY THROAT

by Meriah Crawford

I was supposed to be on vacation. I was supposed to be re-laxing, putting my feet up, reading. I was supposed to be eating locally caught seafood, like drum, soft-shell crab, and oysters dug fresh. I was supposed to be sitting on the porch of my little rental cabin on Chincoteague, enjoying the break I'd earned after nearly four solid months of long hours, seven-day weeks, and living out of my car while working on a huge class-action lawsuit. The phone was not supposed to ring, and if it did I was not supposed to answer. But it did, and I did, and this is what happened.

"Is this Lauren? Lauren Lindsay?"

I could tell from the voice that something was very wrong. "Yes?" I said.

"My name is Harriet Reynolds. I was Jess Walter's college roommate." Jess is a lawyer friend of mine who I work for as a private investigator. She had sometimes referred clients to me, but she also knew how much I needed this time off.

"It's my husband," she said, her voice breaking. "He's — he's missing." Harriet began sobbing.

I could almost feel her body shaking over the phone. I'd had people start crying before — usually while telling me they suspected their husband or wife was cheating on them — but not like this. I waited for a couple of minutes until the storm began to ease, then said, as gently as I could, "I'm so sorry about your husband. Tell me what I can do to help you."

"I want you to find him. *Please.*"

Though I was reluctant to take any new work on, for Jess's sake I decided to at least hear her out. I pulled out a notebook and pen, and sat to take notes.

Tom Reynolds, a retired bank manager, went to visit his mother one afternoon, just over a week earlier. Harriet stayed behind because of a migraine and went to bed early. When she woke up at almost eight the next morning, Tom still hadn't come home. Harriet waited a couple hours and then called his mom, who told her that Tom left just after eleven the night before, saying he was going straight home. Harriet then began a frenzy of phone calling: hospitals, the police, friends and family in the area. Nothing. After another call to Mom, who was starting to get frightened, Harriet drove the route to Mom's house, and then back by a slightly different path. There was no sign of him. Nothing at all.

Later that same day, the police found Tom's car. It was a couple miles off his expected path, which was explained by the fact that the fuel tank was empty. The working theory was that he'd noticed he was low on fuel sometime after he started home, and turned toward the main highway where he knew he could buy gas at that hour. But he'd obviously run out before he got that far. It seemed reasonable to think he'd simply started walking, since it was less than two miles to the nearest gas station. But what happened then was anybody's guess. Finally, after a week's work with no solid leads, the police had admitted that there wasn't much more they could do. And that's when Harriet called me.

I'd worked missing persons cases before, but they were all fairly basic, like finding old friends, or catching up with a rebellious son who'd left home at sixteen and not been heard from since. It was usually a matter of doing a bunch of online searching followed by, at most, a few phone calls. There was one young woman I hadn't been able to find for seven months, but it turned out she'd moved to a different state and lived with friends for a year while saving up to rent an apartment.

But this? I listened to Harriet's story over the phone, and it didn't make much sense to me. It all came back to a simple question: If he wasn't dead, why hadn't he called? There was a time before cell phones, when some rural areas didn't have phone service available for every home, that he might just be sick or hurt and not able to let her know. But the man had a cell phone, as do most people nowadays. It seemed clear to me that he was gone either because he wanted to be, or because he was beyond wanting. Beyond anything. Either way, it wasn't going to end well for Harriet.

After briefly flirting with the idea of declining the case, I suggested we meet to talk in person. Why didn't I just tell her I couldn't do it? I owed it to Jess. Besides, it was an interesting case. I'd like to say I did it because I care, because Harriet's pain touched me. But as much as anything, I just wanted to dig into the case and find the answer for myself.

Harriet gave me directions, and I started off. I hadn't seen much of the Eastern Shore on my drive to Chincoteague because I'd gotten a late start. What I found in daylight was a single north-south highway lined mostly with tiny strip malls and fields of corn, soybeans, and tomatoes. A foul stench announced the presence of the area's other major industry: a chicken processing plant. I slid the window up and put the air on recirculate, trying not to think about the smell and the flocks of seagulls rioting over the back lot.

Away from the commercial areas, on narrow, winding country roads, I saw a mix of farmhouses, mobile homes, and small housing developments sprinkled among fields and a few tracts of wooded land. A nice place to visit and drive through, but rural areas like that always make me feel sorry for the local kids, imagining the boredom they must suffer growing up. And there were so many bleak houses that bore signs of neglect and deep poverty.

It made the small housing development that Harriet had directed me to all the more striking. The Reynolds had a recently built single-story brick house with a view of the Chesapeake Bay between two houses across the road. It was lovely, but utterly silent. There wasn't even the sound of birds. When the houses were built, they must've scraped the land clean. The only landscaping I could see consisted of saplings and clumps of ornamental grass, not dense enough to sustain much in the way of wildlife.

The stillness gave it the feel of a house already in mourning. For her sake, I wished there were a small crowd of family and neighbors there, but during the nearly two hours I was there, the phone didn't ring, and no cars even drove past. It made some sense when she told me they'd just moved to the area to help take care of his mom, but it was still so grim.

I sat quietly and listened to Harriet tell me the story again, encouraging her to add more details or explain when it seemed relevant. She had an easy manner about her, and a gentle, quiet humor that, even in the midst of this nightmare, peeked out now and then. But she was clearly both physically and mentally exhausted, and when she finished she sat and stared silently out the window, as though she lacked the energy to even think of what to say next.

"I'm sorry," I said, "but there's something I have to ask."

"You want to know if he might have left me," she said tonelessly.

I waited for her to continue.

After a moment, she shook her head and turned to look at me. "No." She straightened and gave me the most confident look I'd seen from her so far. "I understand you have to ask that, but I would bet the whole state of Virginia that he'd never cheat on me. Not ever. And Lord knows, he's had opportunity to. Conventions, business trips, late nights at work."

"Then, how . . ." I paused, knowing she could guess what I meant, and we'd both like it better if I didn't need to spell it out.

"Because he tells me everything. He told me the time he got drunk during a conference and called his boss a jackass. He told me when he dented his rental car and told the company he had no idea how it happened. He even told me when his assistant at the bank told him she was in love with him — and he let me decide what to do about it." She nodded to herself at the memory.

If nothing else, she was sure of her man's devotion, and for that, at least, I envied her. I don't know whether it was me, or the men I chose, or simply a reflection of the times, but three of my last four boyfriends had found monogamy too great a burden. Of course it was also possible that she was just in denial. Clients are often wrong, whether willfully or not.

"Okay," I said. "Is there any other reason he might take off without telling you?"

She tilted her head to the side, questioning.

"Like, I don't know, rescuing a friend in distress? Helping a family member he knows you don't like?" I frowned, thinking, grasping for something even remotely plausible, and she stared at me eagerly, hoping for more.

She seemed to realize I had nothing else to suggest, and sat back, looking momentarily numb again. "No," she said. "Nothing like that. I did wonder at first if he ran into someone. Decided to go for a beer and managed to get drunk, then slept on their couch. But of course as that first day wore on, that got less and less likely. And by now . . ."

"You've called everyone?"

"Yes." She rested her hand gently on a stapled stack of papers on the table beside her. "I called everyone I could think of. Everyone in his e-mail contact list who might have heard from him. Nothing. Nothing, nothing, *nothing*." Her fists suddenly clenched, her eyes narrowed, and her lips pressed tightly together.

I kept going, hoping to distract her. I asked about money, his credit cards, retirement accounts, investments. Nothing had been touched. She'd spent considerable time over the past few days going over the last three years' worth of financial data, and nothing seemed amiss. Nothing was missing from the house, as far as she could tell. He didn't even have much money with him. She thought it would have been less than $20, since he rarely carried much cash anymore.

"Oh," I said quickly, "why is that?"

She half smiled. "He'd always be donating money, or loaning it out, or just giving big tips to people wherever he went. I don't mean to sound . . . I mean, I love that about him, that he's so generous, but you see — well, he'd just go through the money so quickly, so we agreed. He carried just enough for a paper, lunch, maybe a few little things, and told everyone his wife had him on a strict allowance." She shrugged, looking uncomfortable. "I suppose people thought I was controlling and cheap, but we really couldn't afford for him to spend so much."

She looked intently at me, as though waiting for my approval, so I said, "Sure, that makes sense." She nodded again, and began shuffling through the papers.

Based on what she showed me, it was clear they were comfortable financially, though not wealthy by any means.

Most of their money was in the house, which was paid for, and their two cars. Kidnapping seemed unlikely but still worth considering. "Had anyone asked either of you for a large loan recently, or seemed particularly interested in your finances?"

"Not so far as I know."

"Since the night he disappeared, especially right afterwards, were there any strange phone calls or hang-ups?"

"No."

"Any odd letters or packages?"

She froze. "Gosh, I don't know. We don't even have a mailbox here. Everything goes to our post office box. I guess someone might have put something in a neighbor's box by mistake."

I asked her to check with the neighbors, glad to have a task to give her, and then I asked for a copy of the contact list. She stood and took it with her to a room down the hall where I heard a copier running.

While she was gone, I scanned the room. It was neat, spare, with a faint haze of dust on everything. The furniture was mostly new in an odd mix of overstuffed upholstery and shaker-style pieces, with a few ornate antiques thrown in. An upright piano stood in one dim corner with a handful of photos scattered across the top. A pleasant room, but it didn't tell me much.

Harriet's shoes — navy leather pumps — thudded faintly as she moved from carpet to wood to rug coming back into the room. She handed me the pages and we sat for almost twenty minutes going through them, page after page.

"He never deletes anyone out, even people he hasn't spoken to in ages. Tom always says that some of his best times are spent talking to old friends and business associates. He can pick up the phone and call someone he hasn't heard from in a decade or more, and talk and laugh and do business with them like they'd played golf that weekend." She smiled, looking almost happy for a moment. "I've never understood how he could do that. I'll run into someone I haven't spoken to in six months and not have a word to say beyond 'how are you' and 'you look wonderful.'"

Harriet showed me the code she used when she went through the list, noting which ones she called, which people he knew only faintly — say through church or Rotary, which were family and close friends, business associates, people she knew he hadn't spoken to in ages. I added a few notes as well, including highlighting people Harriet hadn't been able to locate, and anyone who lived on the peninsula.

After a few more questions, I finished by asking, "Is there anything else you'd like to ask me, or any questions you have?"

She stiffened abruptly and looked down at her feet, and I braced myself. She said, "Do you think he's alive?"

I paused, trying to come up with the right answer, but there just wasn't one. "I really don't know, Harriet."

She sighed and leaned back in the chair, looking exhausted and defeated.

I suggested she get some rest, and promised I'd call within a couple days to give her an update. She nodded dully and sat staring straight ahead while I let myself out. As I climbed in and started my car, I felt as though I'd escaped. I was relieved to be out of there and away from her grief and fear. At the same time, I couldn't help feeling thrilled to be working on such a baffling case. Those emotions together brought a truckload of guilt with them. The only thing I could really do to help her was to find her husband, and I needed enthusiasm to do my job well, but did that excuse it? That was another question I wasn't prepared to answer.

I called the sheriff's office and set up an appointment to meet with Lieutenant Withams, who was surprisingly willing to talk. We met at a nearby Hardees and found a quiet corner to sit in.

"So, what is it you need to know, ma'am?" he asked, a large, rough hand planted firmly on the creased and dirty file folder in front of him.

A full copy of the file would have been nice, but it seemed unlikely. "How about telling me what steps you've taken so far. I'm sure you've been thorough."

He raised his eyebrows. "Are you?"

"Well, I know your time is limited —"

He put a hand up. "Sheriff told me to cooperate, and I will.

I don't need my ego stroked." He started by pulling out a map and folding it into about a twelve-inch square. "Here," he said, making Xs with a blue ballpoint, "is where we found the car, here's his Mom's house, his own home, and the gas station we're guessing he would've headed for."

I studied it briefly, asking questions about the exact spot where Tom's car was. "I was wondering — could he have gone to a nearby farm or something where they might have had some gas to give him?"

Withams shrugged again. "That area's mostly a mix of marsh, housing developments, and fields." He turned the map toward him. "Lots of folks have dogs and shotguns, too. Not to mention jobs to get up for, bright and early. That time of night, I don't see a man like him waking someone up just because he was dumb enough to let his tank run dry. But, who knows?"

I took notes as Withams continued. He had been thorough. He'd spoken with dozens of people, knocked on a lot of doors, checked accounts, cell phone usage, even spoken to a few people at Tom's former job.

"And the car?"

He flipped through the file until he got to a report from the state police, who had more of a crime lab than the local department. "No signs of blood, no tampering or forced entry. Nothing illegal or out of the ordinary at all, in fact. No papers aside from the manual. Missus Reynolds said he'd just cleaned it out, and the garbage all went to the dump. And the scene? No skid marks, no footwear impressions, nothing dropped or discarded." He scowled at it. "Nothing. Just nothing."

He listed a few other things he'd done, including checking Tom's credit and his criminal history, which basically got him nowhere. When he was done, I asked, "Lieutenant, what do you think happened to him?"

He pushed back slightly from the table, and reached down to adjust some piece of gear on his belt. Finally, he sighed and shook his head. "I haven't the slightest idea, ma'am. There is not one piece of this that makes sense to me. It's that *damn* car." He looked up to see how I'd react to the curse, and seemed reassured by the lack of offense on my face. "Well, if it weren't for that, I'd be sure he'd taken off with some lady. As it is?" He shrugged. "I was half expecting him to roll in hung over the next day, or for his wife to get some kind of half-assed redneck ransom note." He looked at me more confidently this time, almost challenging me to object to his words.

I ignored them and went on. "Could he have gotten lost in the woods?"

He exhaled sharply and tilted his head. "I don't see how. He might've forgotten the woods around here since he moved away, but I understand he's been a hunter all his life — and a good one. He'd be too savvy for that."

"Have there been any abductions that look similar to this? Kidnappings?"

"Only on TV," he said. "I'll tell you what we have seen, when adults have disappeared. The person, man or woman, has had some bad news — usually money or health, or maybe a cheating girlfriend — and they've gotten in a car or thumbed a ride on the highway, and they just vanished. Sometimes they turn up again. Sometimes not. But oftentimes there's just no way to find them until they get locked up for something, killed or hurt bad, or . . . hell, one guy — real sumbitch — he sent his wife a postcard from someplace sunny telling her how much happier he was not to have to listen to her whining anymore. As if there was something unreasonable about her expecting him to work now and then and help pay the bills." Lieutenant Withams had a very mean look on his face as he remembered it.

When he turned his attention back to me, I asked, "Is there anything you can recommend I look into? Anything you didn't have time for that might be promising?"

He leaned forward, resting his chin on his folded hands. "Let me see. She gave you the list of contacts?" I nodded. "I called the top tier — the ones he had the most contact with. But there are maybe two hundred more on there that I just didn't have time for." I grimaced, and he smiled. "And I didn't knock on every single door between the gas station and where we found his car."

I sighed and nodded. "Okay, I'll start on those. Will you let me know if you can think of anything else that might be useful?"

"You bet. And if you find anything . . ."

"I'll keep you up to speed." Only with Harriet's permission, that is, but he didn't need to hear that.

I followed the lieutenant to the field where the car had been found. There was nowhere to pull off except for the dirt-and-gravel farm road that Tom had left his car on, and I wanted to leave that clear. The roads were narrow with no shoulder, and edged with deep drainage ditches, so Withams obligingly turned on his lightbar and waved to me to park in front of him along the road. I got out and he showed me the spot, pointing out various landmarks. There was a trio of rusting bins — wide, squat silos made of corrugated steel that farmers store grain and seed in — just visible above the tree-line.

"Those bins —" I started.

"Checked 'em, first thing. Also the abandoned house beyond those trees there," he pointed toward where I knew the bay was, "and the five closest houses."

I walked around for a few minutes, eyes down, studying the ground. There were prints all over, from boots and sneakers mostly, but I knew it had rained heavily early on the morning after Tom had disappeared, so they'd be more recent. I nudged at some trash with my foot, and peered under a plastic bag.

Withams watched with a slightly amused expression. "What are you expecting to find?"

"More than I'd find if I didn't look at all," I said. "I'm sure you already did this, but it never hurts to have another set of eyes."

He shrugged, then walked back to his car and propped himself on the hood.

I kept going, moving in a spiral pattern out from the car's location. I wanted intensely to find some critical piece of evidence. After ten minutes, I'd have settled for finding something mildly interesting or even vaguely suggestive. But aside from a disturbing amount of roadside trash, there was nothing that struck me as deserving to be called evidence.

Finally, as I saw the lieutenant checking his watch, and my own patience began to wane, I gave in and decided to spend the rest of my afternoon knocking on doors. Withams wished me luck, and we drove off in opposite directions.

I went to house after house that day, well into the evening, repeating the same words. "Hi, my name is Lauren Lindsay. I'm a private investigator. I was hired by Harriet Reynolds, from over near Craddockville, to help find her husband, Tom. Do you remember the night he went missing?"

I met some very nice people; some that were polite enough, but probably wouldn't tell me if my butt was on fire; some that didn't seem bright enough — or sober enough — to remember a night eleven days earlier; and a handful that were so creepy that I found myself checking their yards for signs of freshly turned earth or unusually well-fed hogs.

After repeating my spiel yet again, one woman asked, through a barely cracked door, "There a reward?"

I hesitated, and she started to close the door, so I said, "Sure. Yeah, I'm sure that could be arranged. Did you see something?"

"I might have," she said. "Which night was that, again?"

I told her, and she said she saw a man picked up by a maroon sedan, around 11 P.M. "And . . . I think they was fighting."

I got the clear impression she was inventing on the spot in the hope of making some cash, so I asked for a description. The woman hesitated. "Did you see if he had a ponytail?" I asked.

"Oh yes, that's right. I remember he did."

"Thanks, then," I said. "Wrong man."

She slammed the door, swearing, as I turned and walked back to my car. That was the closest I came to anything useful.

And Withams was right — most of the locals did have dogs. I was sniffed and growled and barked at. A gorgeous black lab-rottweiler mix lunged at me so hard that the chain around his neck yanked him off his feet, and he struggled in the mud to stand again, shaking himself. He was more cautious, but continued barking just the same. If I were home in Richmond, I'd have grabbed my pepper spray before wandering through this area.

The next morning, I was awakened by gulls crying, and the

sound of a small boat as it chugged away from the dock. For a moment, I wished I was going with them, but then the wind gusted and blew a wave of rain against the front windows. An awful day for a boat ride, but a perfect day for computer searches. I started with the PI databases, and found little of interest. The database showed the few places they'd lived — they spent nearly thirty-six years in the same house in Charlottesville, Virginia — but I found no criminal records, no bankruptcies, almost nothing of note. He had a hunting and fishing permit, which wasn't a surprise, and it showed his last employment, at the Virginia National Bank. The rest was as expected — family, neighbors, a whole bunch of people the system thought might be related to Tom, but probably weren't.

It was never easy teasing the meaningful data out from the rest, but I saved the report to refer to later, just in case something came up. Often, the database showed unadmitted bankruptcies, a criminal record here or there — it was always more luck than anything when the system could spit that out — and even suggested a spouse or kids that the person had forgotten to mention. But I already knew Harriet and Tom were married, and their data was pretty straightforward. They had no mortgage on their current house, owned no other properties, and there wasn't even a speeding ticket showing.

I moved on to a whole slew of other searches, like newspapers, blogs, and general web searches. I turned up some interesting articles, including a profile of Tom in the *Charlottesville Daily Progress*, published when he retired. I learned that he was an avid golfer, an active member of Rotary and the local chamber of commerce, and had served on the city council for two terms more than ten years earlier.

The other stories that mentioned Tom were related to charity walks, scholarships given by the bank, and the city council — that sort of thing. Harriet's name came up in a few similar articles, though she was less public with her activities. I pulled up one story whose title caught my attention — "Reynolds Indicted for Check Fraud" — but it was Shauna Reynolds, no relation. Her attorney's name was Tom, which is why the article came up. I sighed in disgust and went outside for a quick break.

The overhang on the porch protected me from the slow, light rain, except when the wind carried it in my direction. The air was warm and smelled salty-sweet, and I wished I could walk on the beach. I knew there was a short path I could take to get a closer look at the lighthouse that I could see from the small deck, and there were overlooks where I could see herds of wild ponies and flocks of egrets and ibises. And then maybe some nice, fried local seafood for lunch. I wanted so badly to go out and play.

Over the last few months, I'd taken scores of repetitive statements in a huge class-action lawsuit, picked up medical records, made thousands of copies, written reports, handled stupid questions, and answered phone calls at all hours, and all of it critical, urgent, life-or-death. Then the clients would call with questions that made it obvious they hadn't even read the reports I'd sent them.

I complained to Jess about it — she'd referred the law firm to me — but she was less than sympathetic. "Brainless paperwork and brain-dead clients are part of the gig, darlin'," she told me, and then reminded me how much they were paying. And yeah, that was nice, but I'd barely seen or spoken to friends and family since it started, and as for dating . . . well, I wasn't sure I'd particularly missed that. Still, I wondered if I'd made a mistake by becoming a PI. Is this what my future would be like? I heaved another deep sigh, went back to my desk, and started plugging keywords into the browser again.

By the time the sun began setting and I'd decided to stop for the day, I had a large file of copied web pages on my computer's desktop, a couple pages of written notes, and a half dozen appointments for the following day. I'd called a few people that the lieutenant and Harriet had both already spoken with, just because they were the most likely to hear from Tom: his siblings, his best friends, a nephew in D.C. that he was close with, and some former co-workers. I mostly heard what I expected — a whole lot of nothing — but the nephew, a lobbyist for Verizon, had some interesting insight.

"I dunno," he said thoughtfully. "Aunt Harriet wasn't happy. I mean, she wasn't, like, miserable or anything. But she was . . . like, discontented. You know? And it made him feel guilty?"

"Why was she discontented?"

"Uhhhh." He cleared his throat.

I got the impression he regretted mentioning it, so I said, "I can keep what we discuss confidential. And, really, anything you can tell me might help."

"Yeah. Okay. Well, I guess she wanted kids, but he didn't, so, you know. She loved him. But then, after he retired . . . and it's so quiet out there. She doesn't know anyone, and there's nothing much to do, he told me. But, you know . . ."

"Did he say what he was going to do about it?"

"Oh." I could imagine him shrugging. "He said he'd prob-ably buy her some jewelry or take her on a trip. Something like that. I mean . . . you know, he would never have left. Not *ever*."

I underlined "ever" in my notes, and asked some follow-up questions, but didn't really learn anything else. It was nice that he was so confident about Tom's loyalty to his wife, but people were wrong about that sort of thing all the time. I wanted to believe in Tom, too, but I had to keep an open mind.

The next morning, the sky was still gray, but I was up and ready to roll early. I went to talk with Dan Stockton, the vice president of the local bank where the Reynolds had their accounts. He and Tom had struck up a friendship shortly after he and Harriet first moved there, and they had lunch about once a week. Dan didn't have a lot to say. "We talked about the business world, mostly. He gave me a fair bit of advice, to be honest. Good advice, too. And we talked about stuff like the weather, crop yields, local scandals. That kind of thing. Wish I could help you, but I'm sure I'd be the last person he'd tell if he was planning to take off."

After we talked, Dan showed me details of the Reynolds' accounts, and confirmed that Tom's cards still hadn't been used. Just before we parted company, I asked him the same question I asked everyone I spoke with who knew Tom at all: "Where do you think he is?"

He shook his head. "I've thought and thought about it, and I just don't know. I do *not* know. I'm sorry."

The next few interviews — with neighbors, the president

of their homeowners' association, and even Tom's minister — netted me nothing new except for the revelation that Tom was really fond of root beer, and liked to watch David Letterman after his wife went to bed. Mildly interesting, but not exactly useful.

I ate a late lunch at a shack of a place called Metompkin Seafood, where I had some of the best fish I've ever eaten. I was sitting at a picnic table outside, wiping the last of the meal from my hands, when my cell phone rang. It was Harriet.

I expected a request for an update, or maybe a new bit of information. What I got was some very bad news: Tom's mother, Marian, had had a stroke and died alone sometime late the night before.

"Oh God." Harriet moaned. "I should have been with her. I should have . . . and she died not knowing — not even knowing if her son was dead or alive." She moaned again, harshly. "So help me, if that man just ran off with some woman —" she broke off, said "Damn," and I thought she was going to start crying again.

"Harriet, I'm so sorry." I was especially sorry that I hadn't been able to talk to Tom's mother before she died, though I felt incredibly insensitive even thinking it.

Harriet sighed. "You know, I didn't even like her. I don't know that anyone did, she complained so much. Talked about herself and her troubles all the time. But she loved him dearly. And what a terrible way to die. I didn't . . . I didn't want this. God, I *didn't*."

She said it so insistently that I was certain she *had* wished Tom's mother dead, even if only for a moment, so they'd be free of the obligation to care for her. I felt sorry for Harriet. It's the kind of thought people have just because they're human, without any real desire to see it happen. And the worst of it was, this would make life simpler for Harriet. Part of her had to be relieved that the burden wasn't hers any longer.

We spoke for a few minutes more, and I updated Harriet on my progress. There wasn't much of it, but I hoped it would help her, even if just a little bit, if she knew that I was hard at work.

Once I got off the phone, I headed back to Chincoteague. I

sat and reviewed my notes, hoping I'd see something I'd missed before, but there was nothing. Finally, I pulled out Tom's long list of contacts, scowled at it, and sat down to start dialing. I didn't have high hopes, but I knew from experience that if I worked at it hard enough, sooner or later I'd probably stumble over something useful.

As the afternoon passed into evening, I continued crossing names off the list. I made notes about every call, marked a couple that sounded odd, had numbers that were disconnected, or where I got a machine. By 9 P.M., I was starting to lose steam. I took a break and made a sandwich. While I ate, I stared out at the water, lit by the flash of the lighthouse's warning light rotating in a strange long-short, long-short rhythm. The sight relaxed me, finally, and I decided to call it a night.

It was just past eight the next morning when I started up again, and continued calling for hours. By mid-afternoon, I switched over to the west-coast numbers, which I'd left for last. I was getting ready to dial the fifth California number when I noticed something odd. The man, Ed Gorman, had a Sacramento address, but a Virginia area code — and it looked like an Eastern Shore number. I inhaled sharply, and punched the numbers, thinking, "Be there, be there, be there . . ." Of course, he wasn't. His voicemail answered, and I cursed and hung up.

I went online and did a reverse phone search. The results came on the screen, and I shouted, "*Yes*," when I saw it: 81 Bay Crest Drive, Pungoteague, Virginia. I knew that road name; I'd driven by it the day before. It was near where Tom's car had been found. Less than a quarter mile, and much closer than the gas station, though in the opposite direction. I doubted anyone — myself included — had thought to look there.

I dug in my bag for the map, and tried desperately to think of some explanation that would fit. Tom walked to Gorman's house after the car ran out of gas, and they got drunk together. Maybe Tom had gotten sick or injured, and Gorman was taking care of him.

I unfolded the map, trying to hold onto my desperate, absurd hope, even though I knew it didn't make any sense.

He'd have been home ages ago. But it was too much of a coincidence. It *had* to tie in.

I called the number three more times and finally said, "Screw this," got in the car, and started driving. It would take about fifty minutes to get there. I ran through different scenarios in my mind as I drove, and it started driving me mad, so I cranked up the radio and sang along. There was a song about a guy riding his pony on a boat, and another about tractor love. I was no fan of country music, but it passed the time.

The road Gorman lived on was a smooth gravel track with trees pressing in on either side. The house, no more than a hundred feet back, looked like a fifties-era brick ranch, with large windows and a slate patio out front. There was a light on inside, which seemed like a good sign, but then I saw two packages tucked inside the screen door, and a soggy flyer for a lawn mowing service plastered to the stoop.

I knocked, and for a minute imagined that an amnesiac Tom would answer, looking kindly and confused. But that kind of thing only happens in cheesy soap operas — and it was always the evil twin in disguise, anyway. Neither version of Tom opened the door. After several more attempts and a walk around the house, I had to accept that no one was home.

I walked down the driveway to the road, pulled open the mailbox, and found a note taped inside: "Out of town — family emergency. Please hold mail. Have a blessed day. Lou." At the top was the date the note had been written — three days before Tom had gone missing.

"*Damn.*" I felt like I'd had the wind knocked out of me. After all the work I'd done, this had been my one promising lead.

After a few minutes of staring at the ground feeling sorry for myself, I turned and looked back at the house. It was possible Tom had come here anyway, not knowing they were gone. If he'd arrived on their front steps sometime late that night and found the place empty, what would he have done?

I headed back behind the house, to where I'd seen a shed. Inside, I found a small riding mower, the usual assortment of shovels and rakes, a wheelbarrow, and a few other pieces of equipment. I spotted a gas can under a workbench on the left, and jiggled it. It was full, and I saw no other cans. I suppose he could've taken one with him and walked back to the car. But then what?

There was a garage, too, though. Might they have more gas stored in there? Would Tom know how to get in to check? I started looking around the shed for the key I thought they'd probably have hidden there, not thinking too hard yet about what I'd do if I found it. I lifted coffee cans full of nails, and half-empty bags of grass seed and potting soil. I was getting ready to climb a step ladder and check the beams, when the light shifted, and I heard a man clearing his throat.

I spun toward the door, my heart feeling like it was trying to break out of its cage, and was both relieved and dismayed to find Lieutenant Withams standing there looking amused — mostly.

"We got a call that some girl was sneaking around. From the description, I thought it might be you. Something I can help you find?"

I explained what I'd learned, and why I was at the house.

"Huh," he said, "that was good thinking."

We talked a while, and I was relieved to see he didn't seem particularly upset about what I'd been doing at the house. We discussed the case in detail, and then he asked, "What next?"

I folded my arms and tried to look thoughtful, because it seemed preferable to admitting I had few ideas left. "Did Tom know anyone else down this road?"

"Not so far as I know, though truthfully, I never considered he might walk in this direction. I'd be surprised if he'd take the chance at that hour."

"Maybe he saw it as an opportunity to renew their friendship."

"By asking to borrow gas late at night?"

I shrugged. "Sometimes the best way to get to know someone better is by letting them do you a favor."

He thought about that for a minute and then nodded.

"I tell you what," I said, "I'm going to walk from here to where the car was found, just to see if anything jumps out at me. Come along?"

Withams nodded and called in on his car's radio to let dispatch know where he'd be. We started out walking, and chatted idly about trivial things: the nice weather, the Chincoteague ponies, his fishing trip the month before. I told him about fishing for trout with my dad when I was little. He told me about his grandmother teaching him how to knit, and the fit his father'd had when he came home to find his little man sitting on the couch with his sisters knitting a scarf.

We were both roaring with laughter when I saw it, and it tore the laugh from my throat. It was the underside of a boot, submerged in a deep drainage ditch beside the road, just a short distance from where the car ran out of gas. It might be just an old, discarded boot. It might be nothing. Except for the edge of a black and red flannel shirt that was also floating in the water, in just about the right spot.

Withams noticed I'd stopped, and started to ask what was wrong. But then he saw my face and followed my gaze, and he knew, too. We'd found Tom.

What followed had little to do with me. After they'd removed the body from the ditch, I went with the lieutenant to tell Harriet. She saw us coming up the drive looking grim, and collapsed, wracked with sobs. Her pastor was with her, and he promised he'd look after her. I felt guilty for the relief I felt at being able to walk away, but I could see that Withams felt it, too. I suppose it was natural enough.

I went back to the office with him, answered a few questions, and gave him all my contact information. I made Withams promise to let me know what the medical examiner found, and he said he would. And then, the sun still high in the sky and the day stretching before me, I got in my car and headed back to Chincoteague. If it was a hit and run, it was a matter for the police; if it was accidental — a fall, maybe, or a heart attack — then it was just a shame. In either case, my part in it was done.

I had another week of vacation time left, and suddenly it seemed like a terribly long time. I reached the turn for my rental, and instead kept on driving. Now that I had the time, I was finally going to climb to the top of that lighthouse and see if the view was any better from there.

Meriah Crawford is a private investigator and college professor living in Doswell, Virginia. During a five-month investigation in the Eastern Shore, she learned to love the beautiful and quirky peninsula, and a case she read about in one of the local papers helped inspire this story. Meriah also has an M.F.A. in creative writing from the University of Southern Maine. Her website is http://www.mlcrawford.com

COMPULSIVE BUBBA

by Barb Goffman

My husband could best be described in three words. Compulsive. Abusive. Bubba.

I knew he was compulsive when I married him. Back then, I liked it. Liked how he showed up at my door at the precise moment he'd promised with a red rose in hand. Liked how he always looked as if he'd just whipped his clothes off an ironing board.

Most of all, I liked that he hailed from the South. I'd spent my first ten years in Georgia. Never thought I'd live anywhere else till the day Daddy moved us to Michigan, then up and died in a whiteout on the highway. After Mama remarried and my step-daddy turned out to be a mean drunk, I dreamed of getting out and moving back home. Back South. But I never had the means to do it till Jimmy came along. He dangled marriage and a house in Virginia before my eyes, and I was hooked. The thought of leaving my bad memories and returning to my roots appealed to me mightily. Not to mention, considering what happened to Daddy, I looked forward to never shoveling snow again.

Little did I know.

First time Jimmy hit me, it was snowing. A soft snow, with flakes like little cotton balls raining down from heaven. I hadn't bothered to sweep our front walk before Jimmy came home from work that night. Back in Michigan, we didn't pay no mind to light dustings.

I heard him muttering as the front door opened. His pants were wet, face red.

"It's not enough that I let you stay home all day while I work to pay for this house," were his first coherent words. The word "let" was an interesting one, because my keeping house was Jimmy's idea. He's one of those liberated men who have no problem with wives working, other men's wives that is. I'd been waitressing at a greasy spoon near Jimmy's law school when we met. He liked me serving him. Only him.

"God damn it, Amelia," he yelled. "You made me look bad in the front of the neighbors, letting the driveway get all slippery so I fell down. Look at my pants. They're all dirty! I'm not going to put up with this."

He pulled back his right arm, and before I knew it, his fist landed square in my stomach.

I learned then and there to be mindful of the weather. And to keep both a broom and a shovel handy.

I spent that first night trying to figure out what to do. Didn't want to go back to Mama. My step-daddy wasn't much different from Jimmy. And I couldn't afford my own place. I didn't make any money. Jimmy controlled everything. Even the house was in his name. Then, the next morning, Jimmy was real apologetic. Brought me flowers. Said it'd never happen again. And I bought it.

Guess I inherited denial from Mama.

So I went on cleaning Jimmy's house and pressing his pants. Making sure I had enough beer and chips on hand every Sunday so he and his pals could fill their guts while watching football or baseball or whatever sport was on TV. And I went on feeling my own stomach twist every time the weather turned bad.

Now you might wonder how a man can be both fastidious and a bubba. Turns out it's not that hard. Early in our marriage, Jimmy began going out most nights with the boys. Said it was for business. He'd set up his own law practice and needed to mingle. But I knew better. He loved drinking and telling lewd jokes, but he made sure he looked good doing it. Hell, when your daddy's the county judge, I guess you grow up learning the importance of looking right. That explained why he never hit my face. Wouldn't want to leave evidence for the town gossips.

I should've left him long ago. I know that now. Heck, I knew it that first snowy day. But something always held me back. I didn't have any money. Or I didn't have anywhere to go. Or I was plumb scared to be on my own. It was always some stupid reason.

Mostly, I didn't want our daughter, Charlotte, to grow up in a broken home. She loved Jimmy, and I could take the beatings. I could take 'em for her, like Mama took 'em for me to keep my step-daddy around. Besides, I couldn't blame Jimmy too much. I knew he liked things a certain way and should've tried harder to keep the house just so. By the time Charlotte grew up and moved away, the thought of leaving Jimmy was a dim memory. He was my husband, and a wife stays with her husband, for better or for worse.

Now, I don't want to give the wrong impression. We had a lot of worse, but there also was some better. Jimmy could be very sweet. He always brought home flowers on my birthday. On our anniversary we'd dress up and go out dancing. And Charlotte, well, he just doted on her. When she smiled at him, he seemed to glow from within. And to his credit, he never laid a hand on her. I would've dealt with him years ago if he had.

I guess I would've put up with Jimmy forever if he hadn't made two important changes right about the same time. First, after his daddy passed a couple summers back, Jimmy paid off our mortgage with the inheritance money, so suddenly our monthly expenses dropped way down. With the house paid off and the savings we had in the bank, I really didn't need Jimmy no more. If something happened to him, I could sell his law practice to one of his buddy competitors and make enough to be comfortable.

Second, he took up with Mandy Lee, a waitress at a diner near the main road out of town. I'm pretty sure this was Jimmy's first affair, despite that we'd been married thirty years. Frankly, I think he'd been too scared to stray till then. His daddy was real conservative and wouldn't have put up with rumors of Jimmy running around. A month had barely gone by after the old man's death before Gladys, one of the check-out gals at Food Lion, whispered to me that Jimmy'd been spotted at the Motel Six outside of town with Mandy Lee. She thought I should know. She's sweet that way.

I spent a long time trying to figure out what to do after that. I'd grown used to the beatings. But I wasn't used to being made a fool of in public. I wasn't gonna take it. Suppose I cared about my image as much as Jimmy did about his own.

So I followed Jimmy around for a week. Sly like. I wanted to be positive Gladys was right. Of course she was. Gladys always knows everything. I've always thought her talents are wasted at that supermarket. She should work for the newspaper.

Oh, how my blood boiled when I spotted Jimmy and Mandy Lee making out in the back seat of his truck, parked on a dirt road near the old lumber mill where anybody could see. Especially 'cause she must have reminded him of me, back in the day. Bleached blonde hair. Lot of makeup. And a waitress, too. Not only was he cheating on me, but he'd practically chosen my twin.

What'd she see in him? Couldn't have been nothing but dollar signs. Jimmy's charm only went so far, and he hadn't quite maintained his looks. Sure he dyed his hair and exercised some, but the drink showed in his face and belly. Mandy Lee had to be after him for his money. Our money. Heck, she was twenty-five, he was fifty-five. You do the math.

No way I was gonna let that trampy waitress get her claws on my money. Trying to steal my husband was more than enough.

My first thought was divorce, of course. But given Jimmy's profession and his daddy's lingering influence, I knew Jimmy'd find a way to screw me. Besides, this is a small town, and even though I've lived here over thirty years, I'm still considered an outsider.

Didn't help that Jimmy never let me make my own friends. He liked me home by myself at his beck and call.

I could've just left him, I guess. Packed up and moved in with Charlotte on the other side of the state. Lived in the mountains instead of by the mouth of the Chesapeake Bay. But I'd spent so much time in our house, our paid-off house, I didn't want to leave it. I liked the idea that Charlotte could return to her childhood home at the holidays. That my grandbabies would have memories of the pretty ceramic figurines I sometimes bought and set on the living room mantel, much to Jimmy's wrath. I never got a good deal, he said. Always paid too much. Well, I did some calculating now, and if I took a job working retail, I could afford to keep the house. Plus it'd be nice to have a place to go to everyday instead of staying home with the TV as company. There's only so many talk shows you can watch before your brain starts to cave in.

So that left me with only one choice. I had to kill him.

Not right away mind you. Since I'd just learned of the affair — a fact Gladys would surely tell the world about — if Jimmy died then and there I'd be the prime suspect faster than gossip at a church picnic. No. I had to bide my time. Yet I couldn't wait too long, not with Mandy Lee gunning to replace me.

And I had to come up with a way to make it look like an accident. That wasn't easy. Especially since I was so angry, all I wanted to do was shove a knife in his chest and twist it round and round. Bashing his head in with a snow shovel also crossed my mind. Jimmy's beatings always got worse in the winter. Somehow I never shoveled the walk between the carport and the front door well enough for him.

I was sitting on our living room sofa a few days after I spotted Jimmy and Mandy Lee together, thinking about that snow shovel. And how Daddy died in that whiteout. That's when it came to me.

The plan was so simple it kinda scared me. The only tricky part was the timing. I had to wait till winter and hope we got a big snow storm that started in the evening.

Now you may not approve of my plan, but I kind of think God did, 'cause he sent us that wallop of a storm last year, and early, too. It doesn't often snow a lot in Virginia, especially in December.

Little tingles pricked my arms that morning as I listened to the weather report. A nor'easter was making her way up the coast. The winds were gonna wreck havoc on the bay, they said. Plus, they figured we'd get a good six inches at least, with the snow starting to fall late in the night. That'd be too late for my plan. But I waited all day, hoping the storm would speed up a bit.

By dinner time, the snow still hadn't started. Hopeful, I served Jimmy a meatloaf that I cooked too long. I knew that would piss him off and encourage him to go to the bar as usual, despite the impending storm. Then during the meal I started chattering about Oprah. Lord, he hated Oprah. That ran him out of the house fast and good.

At seven o'clock, about twenty minutes after he fled, the

snow started coming. Unlike that first day he hit me, these were big flakes. Heavy ones. They fell at two inches an hour. I worried that maybe this was too much snow too quick, that God was playing an awful trick on me. If Jimmy paid attention, he might come home early to avoid the bad roads. But I didn't have another plan, and I'd made up my mind to kill him. I wouldn't spend another day being the town laughingstock.

So I got down on my knees, and I prayed. Prayed that Jimmy'd get so caught up with his good old boys that he wouldn't worry about slick roads and wouldn't start weaving up the driveway till his usual time, around eleven. I prayed he'd do the same three-point turn he'd done every night since he built that carport next to the tall bushes twenty years ago, backing in under the awning so in the morning he could hop in and take off fast. And since he'd be drunk, that fancy maneuver would take him several tries and wear him out like always, so he'd snooze in the truck before coming in the house.

I prayed to God, all the while fearing the devil would respond instead.

By nine-thirty I felt a little more confident. Enough snow had fallen, and Jimmy hadn't come home. I grabbed my trusty shovel and headed to the driveway. Over and over I scooped up piles of snow, then hauled 'em to the carport and flung 'em at the edges, until I'd created sort of an oval that Jimmy could fit his truck in. I made sure that I put more snow at the back, so there'd be a good solid mound right by the tail pipe.

Then I made a half-hearted attempt to shovel the walk to the house. I had to make it look like I had shoveled some, but I didn't need to do a good job. Not anymore. I left just enough snow on the walk to encourage Jimmy to nap in the truck, in case he thought of coming straight in. Jimmy hated walking in the snow, especially when his legs weren't that steady. And since it was so cold that night, I reckoned he'd leave the motor running and the heater on while he rested before his stagger to the front door.

I counted on it.

At a little before eleven I slid into the house. Boy, I'd cut it close. Moving all that snow took a lot more time than I'd expected. I shimmied out of my jeans and threw on a flannel nightgown. After shutting the lights, I got in bed and rolled around a bit, so it'd look like I'd been sleeping just in case he came in.

But I had no intention of sleeping.

I planned to watch.

When I heard Jimmy's truck start to rumble up our long driveway, I crept to the window. Since I'd been lying in the dark, my eyes had adjusted, and I could see pretty good outside. The moonlight reflecting off the snow helped, too.

Jimmy weaved back and forth, far more than usual. I didn't realize the driveway would be so icy. Lord, it looked like he might spin out and never make it to the carport. Then he'd leave the truck on the driveway and head on in. Boy, would he be mad then.

I held my breath for what felt like forever. Finally, thank the Lord, Jimmy made it to the carport and started his three-point-turn. The truck skidded a bit more, and I sucked in breath. Funny, even with the plan in motion, I got frightened when I thought he might be hurt. The heart's strange that way.

I almost ran out there to bring him in, but then I remembered Mandy Lee. And the pitying looks I'd been getting all over town. And I thought of all the blows I'd endured these many years. I stayed put.

The truck's tires spun as Jimmy tried to back up. He revved the engine over and over, the truck sliding this way and that. I was sure any moment he'd give up, frustrated. And then he'd come inside and share his anger with me. But just as my fear was settling into my stomach, the truck shot back. Its tail rammed right into the large mound of snow I'd created. Then Jimmy cut the lights. And like a puppet on my string, he stayed put, slumping back in the seat. That was odd, because Jimmy typically crawled in the back for his naps. I guessed he'd drank too much for his stomach to handle even that little bit of motion. Not that it mattered. His being extra drunk worked better for me.

He likely began snoring within two minutes, even before the carbon monoxide began seeping into the truck. I figured the local police would call this an accident. Hell, how was anyone down here supposed to know that snow could clog a tail pipe like that? We hardly ever get big storms.

After I watched Jimmy snooze for thirty minutes without stirring, I crept off to bed. Slept like a baby.

The sun flashed through the window the next morning, shining off all that snow outside. I threw on my heavy coat and snow boots, grabbed my shovel, and headed to the carport. Had to make finding Jimmy look authentic.

"Jimmy!" I called for the benefit of any neighbors who might be out shoveling their walks. "You old fool. What in the world were you thinking sleeping in the truck all night? You could've froze to death."

I pulled open the cab door and let out a scream. Sounded pretty authentic if I do say so myself. Jimmy was pale blue and stiff, eyes closed, his head leaning on his right shoulder. Hard to believe he'd never be able to lay a hand on me again. I ran in the house, called the ambulance. It took 'em a while to make it over. The roads were pretty bad. That worked well for me, cause the snow had started to melt. I hoped the evidence by the tail pipe had begun to disappear, too, but I didn't dare check. Didn't want to leave footprints.

Once the paramedics declared Jimmy dead, they called in the reinforcements. The cops and the medical examiner pulled up together. I stood out on the walk, arms crossed over my chest while the wind whipped through my coat. I pretended not to notice, had to look consumed by my grief.

I gave my story to the cops in between sobs that made it hard for me to breathe. (Thought that would be a nice touch.) I railed at Jimmy for going out into that storm. Was furious that he'd napped in the truck instead of coming in from the cold. If only I hadn't gone to sleep before he got home, if I'd checked on him, maybe I could've saved him.

The medical examiner ambled over from Jimmy and gave me a hard stare. "I'm sorry for your loss, Mrs. Marshall." He paused, pulling on his gray whiskers. "But your husband didn't die from the cold."

"Then what killed him, Harry?" one of the cops asked.

I looked up, trying to appear surprised.

"Well, a number of factors seemed to be at work, and I'll

have to do a full autopsy to be sure, but I'd have to say it was the blow to his head that did him in."

You could've blown me over. "What blow to the head?"

"You probably didn't notice it when you pulled open the door, ma'am," the medical examiner said. "But there's a deep impression on the right side of his head. Looks like someone hit him hard."

I tried to make sense of all this but couldn't. Stunned, I went inside and called Charlotte. Pretty soon the cops took Jimmy away. And then they started asking me questions. When was the last time I saw Jimmy? Did I know anyone who'd want to hurt him? And then, with narrow eyes, they asked, how was our marriage? I'd worked so hard to make it look like an accident, and now someone else had gone off and killed Jimmy, and the cops were looking at me. Lord, maybe the devil had heard my prayers.

Eventually I must have satisfied the cops, 'cause they went off to investigate elsewhere. Probably that bar Jimmy loved so much.

For the rest of the day I sat in the house, confused as all get-out. Jimmy wasn't one to get into fights. The only person he'd ever hit was me. I couldn't make heads or tails of this turn of events. I sure was glad when Charlotte came home late that afternoon. She was a real comfort.

It may sound odd, but I felt angry that someone else had killed Jimmy. I may have wanted him dead, but he was my husband, and if anyone was gonna kill him, it shoulda been me.

I tossed and turned all night, trying to figure out who had done it. And worrying that the cops would come back to snoop over here. Would they figure out I'd tried to kill Jimmy? Would they blame me for the blow to his head?

I got my answer the next morning. The doorbell rang while I was having my second cup of coffee. I thought it was Charlotte, back quick from the florist's. I opened the door and swallowed hard. The sheriff was standing there, the handcuffs on his belt shining in the light.

"Morning, Mrs. Marshall." His voice sounded gruff from tobacco. "I'm here to talk about your husband. May I come in?"

It didn't really seem like a request. I let him in.

The sheriff walked beside me to the living room, looking at me sideways. Then he settled on the couch while I sank into Jimmy's favorite chair. He stared at me and sighed. I began feeling real jumpy and worked hard to stay still.

"My boys have done a lot of investigating in the last twenty-four hours, trying to find out how your husband ended up the way he did."

The sheriff paused and stared at me some more. A lump grew in my throat while I waited him out.

"Do you know a Mandy Lee Roulston?" he asked.

I blinked. They'd found out about the affair, and now they thought I'd struck Jimmy in revenge. And I had no alibi! I'd been home alone shoveling all that snow.

My mind raced while I tried to decide how to plead my case. "Mandy Lee. Well, um, yes, I guess I have heard that name."

The sheriff nodded, staring at the floor. "It looks like she's the one who hit your husband, ma'am. We arrested her late last night." He cleared his throat and stood. "I'm sorry I can't give you any more information right now. Just wanted you to know we'd made an arrest."

And before I could ask any questions, he'd said his good-byes and left. I stood there bug-eyed for a few minutes. They'd arrested Mandy Lee? They weren't after me? It took a bit for the news to sink in, and then I got real happy real fast. The sheriff hadn't been playing coy with me. He probably didn't feel comfortable telling me what had happened. But I knew the important stuff. Jimmy was dead. Mandy Lee'd been arrested. Jimmy would've been proud. Talk about a two-for-one deal.

A half-hour later, Gladys came by to pay a condolence call, and she had no qualms telling me what the sheriff hadn't. Thank goodness Charlotte hadn't come back, so she didn't have to hear the details right then.

Seems Mandy Lee had stopped by the bar that snowy night, and she and Jimmy had words. She was tired of waiting for him. Tired of watching me live like a queen in my nice little house while she continued to serve greasy food to men with grabby hands.

Mandy Lee told Jimmy the time had come to make a choice, and God bless Jimmy, he chose me.

Hearing that made my heart swell. Even after all these years, all the beatings and the affair, in the end he loved me. He picked me. That meant something.

Meant something to Mandy Lee, too. She chased him out of the bar, screaming her head off. Some of the boys followed to watch the show. Jimmy tried to ignore her, but at some point she belittled his manhood. Jimmy turned back and slipped in the snow.

It's hard for me to believe what Gladys said happened next, what with Jimmy caring so much about public appearances. But I guess his anger over looking like a fool clouded his senses.

He hauled off and hit Mandy Lee right in the stomach. She doubled over moaning for a moment, then ran forward, ramming her head into him. Jimmy fell back. And she started kicking him. In his stomach and his legs.

And his head.

The fight didn't last more than a minute before the by-standers broke it up. Mandy Lee stomped off, and Jimmy, humiliated, drove on home. It's a wonder he didn't run off the road. Mandy Lee had kicked him so hard, his brains had banged around his skull and started to turn to mush.

That explained why his truck swerved as he came up the driveway that night. And why he weaved so much during the three-point turn. It wasn't the snow and ice and beer after all. I kept that thought to myself.

Now that slut Mandy Lee's in prison for manslaughter, and I'm living the good life. I got a job at Becky's Hallmark Shop over in Grafton, where they sell the prettiest figurines. I get a twenty percent discount. I've finally made some friends, and I still make it home everyday in time to watch Oprah.

Turns out that years ago, Jimmy bought a heap of life insurance from one of his daddy's pals. He'd wanted to make sure his girls would be taken care of in case anything happened to him, the insurance man told me. And every year like clock work, Jimmy upped the policy. Kind of like an inflation adjustment.

So I only have to work part time. And I have more than

enough money to pay a neighbor boy to shovel the driveway whenever it snows. No way I'm gonna do it.

Yep, Jimmy's gone, but he's still taking care of me. God bless my compulsive bubba.

Barb Goffman is an associate general counsel of a Fortune 500 company and a former newspaper reporter. She lives in Herndon, Virginia. When not playing with her dog, Scout, Barb writes mystery short stories. Her first published mystery work, "Murder at Sleuthfest," was nominated for the Agatha Award in 2006 for best mystery short story. It appeared in *Chesapeake Crimes 2*. Barb also has written an unpublished suspense novel. She is president of the Chesapeake Chapter of Sisters in Crime. She dedicates this story to the first woman she knew whose husband cheated on her. D.M., this one's for you!

PRETTY FRAUDULENT

by Sasscer Hill

Around 3:00 A.M., heat lightning splintered the dark skies over Maryland's Laurel Park Racetrack. Sunny Days paced his stall, apprehensive, receptive to a realm unknown by humans.

A man gripping a short, heavy pipe entered the barn. Horses raised their heads, nostrils flaring at the stranger moving along the stable's dirt aisle. The intruder shoved his way through a stall gate, pausing to study his victim.

The racehorse snorted. His eyes rimmed white, legs scuttling in a backward dance as he retreated to a corner. The man tightened his grasp on the metal pipe and lunged at Sunny Days.

⌐ ⌐ ⌐

I entered the Jockey Club at Laurel Park, journeying back to a world grown distant since Ed's death. I'd pushed through the web of grief that morning, fixing myself up for the first time since my husband's funeral almost seven months earlier.

Ahead, my friend Kate Perkins lounged at a table, a martini glass at her lips. A man, partially hidden by a vase of blood-red roses, sat nearby. As I moved past a table of bettors poring over the *Daily Racing Form* and skirted a crowd studying simulcast monitors, I felt the low hum of gamblers' tension.

A waitress hurried past with a tray. The almost forgotten scents of beer, whiskey, and sliced citrus trailed behind her. I closed my eyes a moment. How Ed and I had loved our before-dinner drink. *Keep going, Janet.*

"Janet Simpson, meet Greg England. He knows *everything* about horses." Kate sounded excited, as if she'd just won a prize. Her head, with its tight perm and pink designer glasses, bobbed in bird-like animation.

The man behind the roses came into focus. Immediately, I understood Kate's enthusiasm. So attractive. Young, maybe thirty-five. Blond, wide-set blue eyes, laugh lines around a full mouth. Something stirred in me, and for a moment the weight gained during the years with Ed bothered me a little. My fingers brushed the knit collar of my gray silk suit, a flattering piece. Why had I worn such sensible shoes?

Greg rose, offering a chair. Kate pushed a racing program across the table, her diamond bangle-bracelets clinking, refracting light like Fourth of July sparklers.

"How fortuitous, running into Greg," Kate said. "You've always wanted to own a racehorse, Janet. Greg's your man. He's in the loop. Buying horses at the Timonium sale next week. For important clients."

"I'm an agent," he said. "I can pick out a good horse for you, arrange for a trainer." He paused a beat. "Whatever you need." His direct gaze was friendly, his smile so infectious I surrendered and smiled back. A prominent, aquiline nose lent him character, making the term "pretty boy" seem inappropriate.

"You should have fun, Janet." Kate's head nodded in affirmation of her own opinion. "Buying a young horse will give you a reason to get up in the morning. You *need* one."

I took a breath. "I've wanted a racehorse since Alysheeba won the Kentucky Derby, but my husband wasn't interested."

"He was too tight to spend the dough," Kate said. "Now it's *your* money."

I stiffened. Kate's wealth came from the rich husband who'd abandoned her for a younger woman. Even so, I didn't like her bitterness spilling onto Ed.

Greg caught my tension and rolled his eyes slightly as if saying, "What can you do?" He flagged a waiter, asking what I'd like to drink. "How'd you two girls meet, anyway?"

"We took the same poetry course and wrote terrible poetry about horses."

"Terrible," Kate said.

Greg pulled a card from his tweed jacket. "I hear you've had a rough time, probably don't want to make snap decisions. Think about it. Call me. I'd like to help you out."

I considered Greg's offer while drinking a ginger ale, picking at a shrimp salad, and watching Kate's bay mare finish third in the fifth. By the time I left, I'd decided.

▟ ▟ ▟

A groom led the roan filly into the early October sun. A white paper pasted on her hindquarter identified the horse as Number 229 in the Fasig-Tipton sale of Thoroughbred yearlings. She looked pretty, but what did I know about conformation, let alone pedigree? At least a dozen animals had paraded before me. One more word from Greg about the shape of pasterns, line of the shoulder, or set of the hock, and my eyes would glaze over.

"It's a lot of information, but I've done the homework for you. Picked out some runners." His fingers slid across my wrist. "You're a trooper, Janet. You've got class. You should have a classy horse." His smile touched me, warm and lazy. "Let me get some coffee and those oatmeal cookies you like."

Perched on a white bench in the warming sun, I wished Greg didn't stir me so much. I'd called him about a horse. He'd taken me to dinner, a wonderful evening. He'd been so thoughtful, so interested, his attention like a sliver of hot sun piercing a crack in a dusty blind.

Time for a mental head shake. I was uncertain about the horses and wouldn't mind more input from Kate. We'd talked on the phone earlier, and I'd asked the obvious question — what's in it for Greg? Kate explained he received a five percent commission.

"Of course," she'd continued, "the more expensive the horse, the more money he gets. But his reputation is top-drawer. Let him make the decisions. He'll find you a winner."

No problem. I'd been raised to rely on men. I studied the horses, barely a year old, led by grooms in khaki pants and caps. The yearlings glowed with health, their manes silky, coats buffed to a high sheen. Glistening hooves suggested pedicures were much in vogue at horse auctions.

A young woman in jeans and leather boots sat on the end of my bench. She placed a large, leather case on the ground and withdrew a long-lens camera. She clicked buttons, rotated the lens, and waited. When a group rounded the corner of a nearby barn, an agent rushed to meet them. He snapped his fingers, and a groom hustled over with a lead shank.

The camera girl rose, shooting pictures rapidly. She focused on a man, his tall frame stooped and sagging. Gray hair, weathered face, and gnarled fingers spoke of life in the elements. He wore an old jacket and English tweed cap. With him stood a man and two women dressed in designer clothes, their hands glittering with diamonds. A horse appeared for their inspection, and the photographer captured the scene, frame by frame. Satisfied with her pictures, she sat down.

I smiled at her. "Should I know who that is?"

"That's Leonard Cushman." Reverence touched the girl's voice.

"I've read about him. Isn't he . . . ?"

"He's like a Hall-of-Fame trainer, three Kentucky Derby winners, this year's Preakness winner. He's awesome."

"So he knows how to pick a winner?"

"Major understatement. Major. Got to go. Good luck." The girl grabbed her bag, trotting after Cushman and his well-heeled entourage.

Greg returned, carrying a cardboard box with coffee and cookies. I grinned. He had my number and didn't mind playing it. But wasn't this business? Greg just doing his job? I bit into an oatmeal cookie, thinking about Golden Drawer, the colt Greg touted. The horse was a head turner, his copper coat and brilliant white socks promising riches down the road. Greg insisted Golden Drawer's pedigree eclipsed most at the sale. Said I could get him for around $40,000. A lot of money. Did the colt carry the potential Greg saw in him?

"What do you think, Janet? I'm leaning toward Golden Drawer. You have a pick?" Greg's glance brushed my face like a caress.

God help me for thinking it, but if I bought the horse, Greg would stay in contact with paperwork, the selection of a trainer, and . . . who knew?

"Let's go for Golden Drawer." My words brought a rush of excitement. I couldn't wait to get into that auction pavilion.

"Great!" he said. "You won't regret it." His mouth eased into a slow grin. His fingers closed around my wrist, the squeeze brief, but startling. "I'll meet you in the pavilion, day after tomorrow, when the sale starts."

He wanted to walk me to my car, but he made me too giddy. "Maybe I'll look around a little more."

Greg blinked once, then smiled. "If you see something you like, just let me check it out."

Nodding, I headed for some different barns, relieved to mosey at my own pace. Not easy, keeping up with Greg's youth and forceful energy. The nearest wooden barn sparkled with fresh paint — gold, red, and white. Bright placards hung outside the stalls, advertising the horses within. Red and gold mums stuffed white planters. The dirt aisles were dampened with water to subdue dust. The scent of wet earth hung in the air. Clearly, the right image attracted money.

A groom paraded a nervous bay colt for two buyers. A cell phone shrilled, causing the colt to rear until almost perpendicular on his hind legs. He twisted, came down, legs churning, ripping the lead from the groom's hands. A half ton of horse with metal-shod hooves headed straight at me. I scrambled backward.

A hand grabbed my arm and jerked me to the side as the horse flashed past, a blur of warm air. Off balance, I fell against the man who helped me. Unmoving strength. The hand on my arm steadied me and pushed me upright.

I turned and saw the weathered face of the trainer who'd so impressed the camera girl. A twitch lifted the corner of his mouth.

"Thanks," I said. "I usually try not to fall on strangers."

"Better you fall on me than under that young hellion." He stuck his hand out. "Leonard Cushman."

I told him my name, feeling the same hard strength in his hand. Figured him for at least 70, yet his eyes were clear, his voice gruff, but strong.

"You all right?" When I nodded, he said, "Shopping or selling?"

"Oh, buying. I think."

The fractious colt, now bug-eyed, charged past us, his frazzled groom struggling to hold the lead shank.

"I don't want one like that."

"He's not happy," said Cushman. "They gotta be happy."

"Happy? I thought you need pedigree and conformation."

Cushman snorted. "These people take their X-rays, shove scopes down wind pipes, stare at legs till they're cross-eyed, and never even look for the horse's heart."

"You mean they should X-ray the heart?"

Cushman threw me a pitying glance. "How long you been in this business?"

"Would you believe a week? I think I need help." Instinctively, I liked this guy. A tough old bird, his face reflected humor and kindness.

"You do need help. Not usually one to hand out free advice, but you . . ." His voice faltered a mini-second. "You remind me of a gal I used to know. You got spunk like her."

His eyes appraised me. "I can see you've got pedigree and good legs and all, but you didn't spit the bit when that colt tried to run you down just now. Showed me heart. You need that in a horse."

He paused a beat. "Course, I look for pedigree, straight legs, clean airways, and all. But it ain't much without heart."

Somehow Cushman imparted more knowledge in two minutes than I'd gotten from Greg in two weeks. "Mr. Cushman . . ."

"I ain't that old, and you ain't that young. Call me Leonard."

"Sure. If I do get a horse, would you . . . train it?" *Where had that come from?*

"Depends on the horse. What are you looking to buy?"

I opened my catalog to Golden Drawer's Hip Number 322. Leonard stooped over further, squinting at the page.

"You don't want that horse."

"I don't?" Disappointment flooded me. I'd been so sure the dam's expensive pedigree would impress.

"His sire, Gold Ring," he pointed a knobby finger to Golden Drawer's father. "Fast as hell. He liked to break on the lead and stay to the wire. But things had to go Ring's way. He got boxed in down on the rail or bumped hard, he'd spit the bit. Most of his foals inherit the speed *and* the chicken heart."

I grew quiet. My lack of experience in this business overwhelmed me. Leonard's mind reached beyond the printed page, poking into past performances and family characteristics, searching for that elusive quality he called "heart."

"What *do* I want?"

Leonard pulled a pen from his tweed jacket, took my catalog, and paged into it. He studied a moment, then wrote some hip numbers on the inside cover.

"Look at these horses. See one you like, go ahead and get it. They've got my number in the Laurel racing office. Call me. Nice meeting you, Janet."

The afternoon shifted toward evening, the activity around the barns slowing. The air cooled, and I shrugged into the black sweater I'd stuffed in my tote. Leonard's four hip numbers were different from Greg's picks, the agents' names unfamiliar. Time to check them out.

The first two were attractive bay colts, but uninspiring. Did I need inspiration? The third horse, a gray gelding, pinned his ears and tried to bite me when I got too close. Not him either. Maybe I should stick with Greg.

Dusk settled on the barns. The scent of summer grass and sweet molasses rode the evening air as grooms replenished hay and scooped grain into feed tubs. They shut wooden doors over wire stall gates. In the remaining open stalls, yearlings hid in the back, avoiding appraising eyes. I peeked through some gates, surprised to see a wrinkled exhaustion about the yearlings' eyes. I headed to see Leonard's last pick.

The barn had a single light shining from an office at the far end. Hurrying along, I took a bad step, stumbled, and dropped my program. I leaned over, grabbed it, and straightened. A chestnut head with a white blaze materialized over the stall door beside me.

This horse was so perky! Big, wide-set eyes with lashes like a girl. The yearling leaned toward me, eyes curious and bright with intelligence. Nostrils snuffled me. I stood there with a pink velvet nose pressed into my shoulder and fell in love.

"You wan me bring her out?" A slim Latino male had appeared and waited for my answer.

Her. Of course. Eyes like that could only belong to a female. I hadn't come to look at this horse. With something like heartbreak, I said, "Actually, I'm looking for Hip Number 77."

"You wan the filly, papa is Platinum, mama is Pearl Drop?" When I nodded, he said, "Is this one."

"Bring her out."

The filly pretty much led the groom from the stall, looking around with great interest, as if she had places to go and things to do. I found her bold and beautiful. Thought maybe I'd name her Platinum Pearl. Knew she was the one.

🪶 🪶 🪶

The next day, I sat opposite Kate in a red leather booth. Behind her pink lenses, tears spilled from her eyes. Her words reduced the noisy Laurel restaurant to a background murmur.

"I don't know how he could have injured himself so horribly. His fractured leg was so severe, the vet had to put him down. Greg told me this morning." Kate's tight perm dipped as she dug into her purse for a tissue.

She'd bought the horse recently, never had a chance to see him run. Now he was dead. I closed my eyes. Hard to escape death.

Something bothered me. "So your trainer didn't call you?"

"No. Greg handles everything for me and, of course, he'd be the one to call."

"Anybody know what happened?"

"Greg didn't say. But, bless him, he made sure I had an insurance policy." Her voice hitched. "But I don't care about the $70,000. I just want Sunny Days."

Our waiter rushed at us, plunking down the whiskey and vodka we'd ordered. Beer glasses for another table dripped white foam onto his tray. Around us, ice rattled in glasses, silverware played on china, and the chorus of conversation swelled.

I hadn't tasted my vodka yet. It would be my first drink since Ed's death. I'd been so afraid of becoming one of those widows who rely on a bottle, I'd avoided the stuff. Unconcerned by such thoughts, Kate reached for her whiskey and took a long sip.

"I saw Sunny two days ago, fed him peppermints and carrots. This is really hard." The pain in Kate's voice was palpable.

Our waiter reappeared. Kate asked for another drink, saying she wasn't hungry. I asked for a salad, wondering if Kate drank too much. Relied too heavily on Greg.

"So did you and Greg buy Sunny Days at a sale?"

"Greg purchased him privately. Had him vetted for me, took care of the insurance."

"He makes it very convenient, doesn't he?" I said. I wanted more involvement. Too many years where first my father, then Ed, made the decisions. Why shouldn't I research the horses? Reach my own conclusion?

"Don't know what I could have done without Greg," Kate went on. "So concerned about me, and sweet."

I wasn't the only one succumbing to Greg's good looks and flattering ways. "Kate, was Sunny Days a good horse? Had he won many races?"

"He was still a maiden."

I might not know much, but five seemed old to have never won a race. "A five-year-old *maiden*?"

Uncertainty clouded her face.

"Kate, if you want to get back on the horse, so to speak, there's a couple I might bid on tomorrow. Maybe we could go in on one together?"

Kate swallowed some whiskey. "I like the idea. But I'd still want to run the horse by Greg."

𝕽 𝕽 𝕽

The next morning, I stood beside the sandwich counter in the back of the sales pavilion while waiting for Kate. A concrete floor with theater-style seating sloped down to a small, dirt-filled sales ring. During the two-day sale, the yearlings would be led inside, one at a time, and sold to the highest bidder. A tall, wooden stand for the auctioneers rose behind the ring.

Close by, a full bar dwarfed the sandwich counter. No doubt the sales company favored customers with money to burn and a fondness for alcohol. I envisioned Kate raising her glass, raising her hand. Maybe I should do the bidding.

Greg emerged through a side door near the bar. No denying the physical rush of excitement. That blond hair, the narrow waist, those long legs.

His face lit with pleasure. "Morning, dear. Ready to bid on Golden Drawer tomorrow?"

"Absolutely. Unless I buy Number 77 today."

His charm faltered. "I don't remember us looking at 77. Have you got the right number?"

"Yes. An adorable filly I found late the other day." A vague reluctance kept me from mentioning Leonard Cushman.

"Janet, your enthusiasm is admirable, but 'adorable' won't cut it." His voice, tight and sharp.

I took a half-step back, staring at him.

He softened, placing warm fingers on my arm. "Hey," he said, "this is a tough business. I just want to guide you." His voice caressed, and an electric response jolted me. I felt . . . young.

I took a breath. "I'm still interested in Golden Drawer. Who's to say I can't buy two horses?"

He paused and looked away for a moment, turned back, his blue eyes warm and amused. "I know better than to get in the way of a beautiful woman and what she wants."

My face felt warm. *Get a grip.* This man wasn't interested in me that way.

"Let me take a look at her for you. I could help with the bidding."

"Great," I said. But I'd found her, not Greg. Almost wished he'd butt out. My heart had responded to this filly, and bidding sounded exciting. I remembered Ed's enthusiasm for buying real estate, closing a deal. I wanted to experience that high, yet I knew Greg expected me to yield on this. I forced a smile, told him I'd wait for Kate, watched him leave to examine the Platinum filly.

Customers wandered into the pavilion, reading posted ads, snapping up handouts strewn on metal tables, greeting acquaintances. I found a quiet corner and pulled out my cell phone, punching in Leonard's number. His rough voice reached my ear, and I told him I liked Number 77.

"You looked at them all? She's your first pick?"

"Yes. I kind of fell for her."

He paused a beat. "So did I. She's special. You saw it, too."

"I'm going to bid on her." When had I decided that? "You'll train her?"

"Yes, ma'am. You ever bid before?"

"No."

"Shysters out there'll bid a horse higher than it's worth. Pick your price, stick to it. Keep a poker face."

"What would you pay?"

"I wouldn't go more than $30,000, but I think you can get her for less."

I felt keyed up. "I want that filly." Enthusiasm sharpened my tone.

"You stay calm. Don't let that auctioneer push you. No reason you can't slow the bidding. Ask a spotter if the numbers get confusing."

"Spotter?"

A pained silence. "The guys on the floor that take bids. Don't be afraid to ask if the bid on the floor is yours or somebody else's. Otherwise, you might bid against yourself."

"Oh."

"Let me know how you make out." He disconnected.

Kate waved from the bar. Her pink fur vest matched the ruff on her short boots. As she joined me, I tried not to gawk at the enormous pink diamond on her right hand. I almost felt sorry for her ex.

I waded in. "Greg's looking at that filly I told you about, by Platinum. Do we really need his approval to buy her?"

She frowned and pursed her lips, so I explained about Leonard. Kate remained dubious.

I shrugged. "Greg loves this colt named Golden Drawer."

"That's the one. I'll go in on him."

Greg returned, a frown on his face. "I didn't like the filly, Janet. I know this business. That is not a horse you'll do well with. Trust me. There are better horses here."

Kate sidled up to him, drawing him into conversation.

I eased away, my disappointment evolving into annoyance. I surprised myself and marched into the sales office where I arranged for credit. I felt defiant and liked it.

Leaving the office with lighter steps, I moved outside the pavilion, stopping abruptly. Greg stood in the parking lot in conversation with a man. The guy was thin, wore a ponytail, and black cowboy boots. His hand gestures were sharp.

Greg's usually generous mouth was compressed, his eye's dark and narrow. Their voices were too low to make out the words, but their tension came through loud and clear.

Greg spotted me and looked away. The other man stared, his face gaunt and unhealthy. He spun his pointed boots and moved off between some cars. When Greg turned back, his "pretty" face was in place.

🐾 🐾 🐾

Hanging in the back of the sales pavilion, I tried to keep a low profile and concentrate on the auction. Another yearling skittered into the sales ring, staring in apparent terror at the bright lights and mob of humans. The microphone blared, the colt whinnied frantically, his groom working hard to keep him moving in a controlled circle.

The auctioneer's voice cracked like a whip, driving the bidding to a frenzied pace. Hard enough to follow the rising dollar amounts. The rest of the man's chant sounded like gibberish. Without warning, his rhythm slowed.

"I have twenty-four, five. Do I hear twenty-five thousand?" He looked around the room. The spotters gave their bidders a last hard stare. The hammer dropped. "Twenty-four, five."

The horse moved out, and the auctioneer began touting the next entry, Number 75. How had that happened so fast? My filly was practically next. I felt the touch of someone's stare. There, down near the sales ring, Greg's eyes. On me. I pretended I hadn't seen him, wished he hadn't walked in.

"Hip Number 76 is out," the auctioneer said. "Hip Number 77 is the chestnut filly by Platinum, out of Pearl Drop. Who'll give me $2,500?"

Oh, my God. With a rush of adrenalin, my heart hammered to the auctioneer's rising song. Tentatively, I raised my hand. A spotter caught the movement, and his eyes locked onto me like heat-seeking missiles. My bid whirled away into the vortex, and the price shot up to $15,500, then hesitated. I raised my hand for $16,000. The bidding flew to $18,000 and stalled again. The next call sounded final. I nodded at the spotter. Seconds later, the hammer dropped, and the auctioneer said, "$18,500, to the lady in the back."

🐾 🐾 🐾

I handed Kate a Dunkin' Donuts bag and sank gratefully into the Lincoln Town Car's heated leather. The early morning carried a damp chill, making the scent of fresh coffee and warm fried pastry irresistible. As Kate organized napkins and cups, my thoughts slid to the previous afternoon.

I'd arranged for the filly's transportation to a training farm, then struggled through a "wish-I-could-tell-Ed" reflex. Mostly, I hadn't been able to shake this weird feeling about Greg. A half-formed idea had uncoiled in my head; I hoped it was way off base.

I glanced at Kate. "Why does Greg push so hard for *his* picks? If he'd bid on the Platinum filly, he'd still have gotten five percent. Right?"

Kate swallowed some coffee. "Yes."

"Then why didn't he? Feels like there's something extra attached to his picks, like he's got a side deal going."

"No. Your imagination's working overtime." Kate's fingers tightened around her Styrofoam cup, popping the lid off. Coffee splashed over the edge.

Outside the fogged-over windshield, morning traffic clogged York Road. Beyond the snarl of cars a chain-link fence rose, the pavilion looming behind. Barns in the distance stirred as yearlings appeared for inspection by early-bird shoppers.

I turned back to Kate. "Greg's so determined to sell us Golden Drawer. Something feels off."

She dabbed a napkin where the coffee had spilled onto her hand. "He doesn't have some kind of deal going. It would be unethical."

I let that hang in the air a beat. "I saw Greg in the parking lot with a man who looked like a thug. A real creep. Why would Greg do business with a guy like that?"

Behind her thick lenses, Kate's magnified eyes widened. "Greg might not even know the man. It's probably one of those unsavory characters that ask for money. A drug addict or something."

Maybe she was right. Yet . . . "Don't you ever feel Greg's a little too smooth and glib?"

Kate's gaze slid away from me. "What do you mean?"

"He's almost like a con artist, Kate. I'm going to tell him I don't want Golden Drawer."

"Oh." Kate still fooled with her napkin. "I don't want to buy without a partner. Could you tell him I'm out, too?" The frayed paper fell in pieces from her hand.

☞ ☞ ☞

We found Greg outside the Fasig-Tipton sales office. Kate hung a few steps back as I moved toward him. His face brightened with that lovely smile. "How are my girls this morning?"

"Fine." Nerves tightened my throat. "Greg, we've decided not to buy Golden Drawer."

A frown shadowed his face, replaced by a tight smile. "We've come so far together." He stepped closer. "Don't get cold feet now. You're missing a fabulous opportunity." He placed a hand on Kate's shoulder, and she all but fluttered.

I needed to get her away from him before she caved. Her eyes had that hungry baby-bird look.

"Afraid we've decided, Greg. You've been so generous with your time. It's much appreciated. We'll be back in the future." Felt like I was babbling. Maybe because his stare had turned so cold.

I tugged at Kate's hand, moving us away. Outside the auction pavilion, some friends waylaid Kate. Greg emerged, walking past me without a glance. Apparently, I'd become invisible.

I took a breath. I'd go see my filly once more before she shipped to the farm. Maybe her happy nature would lighten my mood. Kate's too. After her friends drifted into the pavilion, we headed for Pearl's barn. I spotted that white blaze. As we drew closer, her ears pricked toward us, nostrils widening.

Someone stood near her head, and it wasn't her groom, Juan.

"That's the guy who was with Greg." Drawing closer, I could see his arms were stained with reptilian tattoos. Was he wearing a rubber glove? Holding a hypodermic syringe? I surged forward, Kate on my heels.

"Hey," I called. "What are you doing?" I broke into a jog. The guy glanced at me, annoyed, like maybe I was a gnat. His thumb moved to the syringe's plunger, his other hand snaking to the filly's halter.

"Don't touch her," I yelled.

"God. What's he . . ." Kate's voice wavered behind me.

A man burst around the far corner of the barn. *Greg.* He sprinted toward the tattoo guy. "Dean. What the hell you doing?"

The guy jerked toward Greg. "You said these women was buying into it. I was getting the money. These bitches don't want your golden horse."

Greg's cheeks spotted red. He edged closer to Dean. "Shut up."

"Shouldn't have cut me out of that other deal. I take care of that Sunny horse for $500 and you get $70,000? That's bullshit."

Kate's breath sucked in. "Seventy thousand?" She clutched my arm. "That's what Sunny Days was insured for."

Dean howled with laughter. "Think you're gonna see a penny of that, lady? Shoulda read that policy Marty here got for you. Have you met Marty Gregerson?" He gestured at Greg. "Also known as England Gregwin. When this boy leaves town, he's gone for good." Dean appeared high on something, out of control. "Man, you find the dumb ones, Marty."

"I said SHUT UP!" Greg grabbed for the syringe.

Dean snapped it back toward Pearl. "Got your prints all over," he sang, waving the hypo at Greg. "You going down, asshole." A sick smile distorted his lips. He turned, grasped Pearl's halter, and swung the needle at her neck.

I threw myself at Dean as Greg kicked him in the side of a knee. Dean and his snake tattoos went down, the syringe flying into the dirt. I ended up on my hands and knees and scooted sideways to get away from Dean. Juan appeared, shouting in Spanish, and two more grooms ran toward us. Dean lurched to his feet, his expression suddenly wary. He took off running.

I wanted to know what was in that syringe. I reached for it, but Greg beat me to it. He grabbed it, bent the needle in half on the heel of his shoe and made the syringe disappear into his pocket.

Platinum Pearl spun in her stall, a small tornado. Juan slid inside, crooning and soothing. Kate helped me to my feet.

I turned on Greg. "You're scum. What, you kill horses for insurance money?"

Anger twisted his face. I backed away, but he darted forward and caught my wrist. It *hurt*.

"Listen, bitch. Think I like sucking up to you old women?"

Rage boiled in my stomach. My free hand swung back, flew forward, and slapped his face. I'd never done that before. It stung. Greg dropped my wrist and pressed his hand to his cheek. He looked more shocked than angry.

Next to me, Kate's voice broke. "You used me . . . took my money."

My jaw felt tight enough to crack. "How much money have you ripped off? How many dead horses . . ."

"You can't prove anything."

"I bet the insurance company can."

Greg's bravado ebbed, the color draining from his face. He eased away, disappearing around the corner of the barn. I couldn't hold him till the cavalry arrived and I wasn't an avenging angel type. Kate could file a police report. Let the insurance companies and legal system have a go at him.

I exhaled a long breath. Heard Kate crying. Pictured Sunny dead.

Greg would shed his name again and set up shop somewhere else. Kill more horses. Leave other women feeling old, foolish, and discarded.

No. I'd find a way to stop him.

I never did like a pretty boy.

Sasscer Hill has recently completed "Venom," the second story in the Janet Simpson series. Hill's short mystery, "Game," featuring young female jockey Nicky Latrelle, appeared in a recent issue of *The Advocate*.

Currently, Hill is working on a novel-length Latrelle mysteries series. Her books *Full Mortality* and *Racing from Death* are under agent contract and in negotiation for publication.

Hill lives on a Maryland farm and has been involved in breeding and selling racehorses for over twenty years. A number of her articles have appeared in the *Mid-Atlantic Thoroughbred*.

THE SERPENT'S TOOTH

by Mary Ellen Hughes

Why did Uncle Harold have to go and get married? All it did, in my opinion, was complicate his life — and force me to contemplate murder.

There he was, a confirmed bachelor and aging rapidly. I was his only living relative and certain to inherit that nice pile of money he'd accumulated over the years from his booming restaurant business, not to mention the nice pile of bricks he'd put up on that extremely valuable waterfront property on the Chesapeake Bay. It would have all come to me, and, considering the condition of his heart, fairly soon. Which, considering the state of my own finances, and the escalating insistence of certain bill collectors, was a situation intensely to be desired.

But then he'd up and gotten married.

They'd met, I was told, in their cardiologist's waiting room where they apparently began sharing stories about surgeries and other geriatric pleasantries like arthritic joints and constipation woes, and, as such things can't help but lead to, fell in love.

"Why marry?" I'd croaked out when Uncle Harold informed me of his plans. I was desperately searching for a way to salvage my dreams. "Why not just live together? That way you'll both keep your social security."

Uncle Harold had chuckled roundly. "Esta won't need her social security. I'll be able to cover any losses in that department."

Yes, but what about *my* loss, I wanted to cry, but was interrupted by Uncle Harold's adding, "This is my last chance for marriage, you know. I've waited much too long, and I may not be around much longer."

That, of course, had been my expectation. I groaned internally as visions of greenbacks flapping away on bridal-white wings made me light-headed. My only hope was to convince Uncle Harold to make a will, something he'd never gotten around to before. A will that would, obviously, name me, being his only blood relative, as the principle beneficiary. I was willing to permit a modest allowance for Esta to live on, but definitely nothing too significant, and absolutely something I could reduce in time.

It was not to be, however. Uncle Harold couldn't be persuaded to take the time during the tizzy of their elaborate wedding plans (imagine my joy to see caviar on the menu — every cracker-dab certain to take huge bites out of my future income.) Then Esta wanted an extended honeymoon in Hawaii, though I pointed out — completely reasonably, I thought — that the bay water that fronted Uncle Harold's estate was just as wet as the Pacific Ocean and would save on the exhausting — and expensive — travel across four time zones.

That exhaustion, it turned out, was not overstated. Before I could drag Uncle Harold to his lawyer's on their return, he took a sudden turn for the worse from a bug he'd picked up somewhere between here and Waikiki, and kicked off. I was not to be consoled! No one wept more buckets of tears at his funeral than I. All that money, that fabulous estate! All was now in Esta's hands for her lifetime, since on his deathbed Uncle Harry had managed to gasp out that particular plan to his lawyer. The lawyer, acting with unprecedented, and, in my opinion unwarranted, speed, had drawn it all up to be signed and legal, including the caveat that on Esta's death everything would then pass on to me.

So, of course I began thinking of murder.

I first took a little time to get to know Esta better, and found she was not the epitome of sophistication. Gullible would be the word for her, and while I worried she might fritter away Uncle Harold's savings through the endless barrage of sob-storied charities that zero in on rich widows like heat-seeking missiles, (my occasional borrowing of a thousand or two to keep the wolf from the door excepted, of course), I also realized I could use her credulousness to my advantage.

During one of our many meals together — shared at Uncle Harold's table which, besides being deliciously prepared by Uncle Harold's faithful old cook, was more importantly, free — I casually asked if she had ever spotted Chessie.

At Esta's puzzled look I explained the legend of Chessie, who was purported to be a cousin of sorts to the famous Loch Ness monster but dwelling in our own Chesapeake Bay. Having lived the bulk of her life in one of those land-locked fly-over states, Esta had never heard of Chessie and she begged for more details. I explained that while not that much was known about the creature, since he — or she — was so elusive, people had certainly seen it, and a blurry photograph or two existed.

"But the water beyond these very bluffs is where Chessie was most seen, Aunt Esta," I lied. "Wouldn't it be exciting to see him yourself?"

Esta's face took on the look of a six year old who believed she might actually get that white, silky-maned pony if she was very, very good. Esta, I had deciphered, retained a childish desire for her own fifteen minutes of fame. What better way (and requiring less actual effort of intellect) than spotting and then snagging the first good photograph of the elusive Chessie?

But first she demurred. "Oh, I don't know. My doctor advises me to avoid too much excitement, which is why these little dinners with you have been so perfect for me." I managed to smile. "But then," her voice grew suddenly husky, "to actually see such a creature!" My smile then grew genuine as I saw that the seed I'd planted had taken root. Over the next few days I watched it grow as I watered it with bits of local folk lore mixed with a few creative touches of my own.

"They say," I told her once, "that Chessie is absolutely bonkers about crabs, which is why he hangs around so steadfastly in the bay. Warnings have even been passed down among the watermen to get their catch back to shore before darkness falls, or Chessie will loom up to devour their day's haul, possibly drowning a crewman or two in the process."

"Ohhh," Esta cried, her eyes round as a child's relishing every fearful/wonderful moment of a scary story.

Another time I advised her to set up flood lights to shine on the water below Uncle Harold's bluffs, since the lights helped the crabs to flourish, and crabs, of course, would attract the sea monster. Total nonsense, of course, but Esta didn't know that. Esta kept pretty much to herself, living at Uncle Harold's estate, and her only companion — the old cook — was so hard of hearing that she wouldn't have understood Esta's questions on the subject if she'd thought to ask them. Esta immediately ordered the flood lights, which fit into my plan perfectly.

I then helped her to choose the proper camera, and worked with her on the operation of it, watching, the whole time, as her excited anticipation grew. Things were progressing nicely on that end, so I began the necessary work on my end, constructing a floating sea monster that would really excite Esta.

To death.

The base would be a simple boat, just large enough to hold me as I paddled slowly past the bluffs. But the neck and head needed to look as realistic and fearsome as possible. I, therefore, spent the bulk of my effort on that, resurrecting skills I hadn't thought of since middle school art class when Mrs. Hickenlooper dragged us through the joys of papier-mâché. Who would have guessed, back then, that Mrs. Hickenlooper, with her dreary, plodding approach to creativity, was in fact providing me a most innovative means of garnering untold wealth. And I hadn't even gotten an A in the class.

The monster was built, and the big day arrived. Esta had begun spending her evenings on the bluff, wrapped in blankets, floodlights on and camera at hand as she scanned the waters below, watching and waiting for her big moment. The weather was clear. Water traffic in the area was low at this time of year, and I pushed off from around the bend in my floating Chessie-mobile, paddling ever-so-silently toward Esta's floodlights.

All was going well. I was inordinately proud of my floating creation. The inflatable black snake-like loops I pulled behind me looked realistically sea-serpentish, and Chessie's head as it entered the spotlight glowed with a fierce beauty. I thought I understood how the Vikings must have felt when their glorious vessels approached the shores of their next victims, spreading terror among the local peasantry. I wasn't looking for terror from Esta, but the kind of excitement that would be nearly as heart stirring. And heart stopping.

I looked up and saw Esta's figure leaping up from her chair, blankets falling away like scales and camera swinging wildly. I had no fear of an incriminating record of my clever caper being captured on that camera, since I had taken the precaution of leaving out one or two vital steps when I'd instructed Esta in her new toy.

Any minute now, I thought, Esta's feeble ticker would give out from the stress. She would fall to the ground, the apparent victim of her own folly, to be discovered eventually by her aged cook. By the time ambulances had been called, and final pronouncements of death made, I would have pulled "Chessie" safely ashore, deflated his body, hidden his head in the brush, and speedily booked to my all-too-humble abode where I would receive the sad news of my having finally inherited millions.

Except:

Chessie started taking on water.

I realized too late that I should have spent more time making my sea-monster sea-worthy.

Before I knew it I was in the water, floundering wildly as I flailed about for anything to keep me afloat.

The last thing I remember is Chessie's fiercely beautiful papier-mâché head, the head I'd been so proud of, bobbing up and down over me as his loopy body flopped and flipped in the waves, my arms reaching desperately to grab anything buoyant and sturdy enough to hold onto but failing, my screams of frustration finally ending in . . .

ɼ ɼ ɼ

"Well, the old girl was lucky she kept her nitro pills with her." Sheriff Webb lit up his pipe as he leaned back in his chair, the coiled spring creaking despite repeated squirts of WD-40. He had just shared the Coast Guard's report with his deputy, Jack Beall. They had pulled up a bizarre, soggy papier-mâché head along with limp lengths of black rubber tubing during their quest to recover the body of Harold Quincy's nephew.

"So she really did see something out there?"

"Yup, just not what she thought she did. We'll never convince her otherwise, though."

"She still thinks she saw Chessie, then?"

The sheriff exhaled a lungful of smoke in a long sigh. "That she does. Chessie, attacking that idiot nephew as though he were some giant crab. That's how she put it, except for the idiot part." Sheriff Webb closed his eyes and recalled Esta, muffled with shawls and pillows as she reclined on her sofa, a silver tea set on the table before her.

"Chessie thought he was a great big crab," she insisted, her eyes round and wide with memories of the horror. "It was the floodlights! They must have confused him."

"Ma'am, what was your nephew doing out there at that time of night, do you suppose?"

"Why," she'd said, stopping as though that question hadn't occurred to her until that very moment, "why, I suppose he must have gone for a swim. Although, it *was* rather chilly, wasn't it?"

She'd lowered her voice conspiratorially to add, "Just between you and me, sheriff, he wasn't terribly bright."

Esta watched the sheriff closely to gauge his reaction. He was buying it, she could tell. Not that Harold's nephew had been out for a swim, of course, but buying that she, Esta, believed that to be the case. As well as believing there had actually been a sea monster out there.

Esta had always found it useful to pretend to be a little less bright than she actually was. And in Harold's nephew's case, a lot less bright. That young man had been getting to be a real drain, in more ways than one. Esta had soon realized she'd have him leeching off her the rest of her life if she didn't do something about it. Fortunately, he had arranged that himself, coming up with that ridiculous plan to get rid of her.

Any fool could have told him it would end in disaster. Of course, Esta wasn't a fool — so she hadn't told him.

She smiled coyly at the tall, strapping man before her. "Tea, sheriff?"

Mary Ellen Hughes is the author of the Craft Corner mystery series (Berkley Prime Crime), which features Jo McAllister — arts and crafts shop owner and resident sleuth of Abbotsville, Maryland. The series began with *Wreath of Deception*, (2006), followed by *String of Lies* (2007), with the third installment, *Paper-Thin Alibi*, to be released in July, 2008. One of her short stories appeared in the first Chesapeake Crimes anthology, with others published in various mystery magazines.

Mary Ellen lives in Anne Arundel County, Maryland, safely inland from the Chesapeake Bay, where she's happy to say the serpents tend to keep their distance. You can learn more about Mary Ellen's books on http://www.maryellenhughes.com.

MURDER AT ELK NECK

By K. B. Inglee

September 1781

The soldier lay between the bushes and the water on the point of land where Big Elk Creek and Little Elk Creek joined and flowed into the Chesapeake Bay. Joanna Clark thought he might be sleeping off a drunk, so she moved away. Turning her head to avoid a branch, she saw what she had not seen before. Blood spread out over the rock he rested on and sank into the sand. Flies swarmed and buzzed around his head.

His white coat with green lapel and cuff told her he was French. He lay face down with his right hand stretched out as though in his last moments he had reached for something just beyond his grasp.

It was already midmorning and she still had to find her missing sheep. Now she would have to go to the French camp, as well. It would be time to eat before she would be able to start the midday meal.

The Continental and French armies had been encamped at Head of Elk waiting for the ships that would take them to Yorktown to face the British. Twice in this war, the little community had been called upon to support the armies. Joanna had been a girl of fourteen when the British troops sailed up the bay to meet the Continental Army along the Brandywine River. During this long hard war she had grown into a woman. Now the Continental Army and its French allies were here.

⌐ ⌐ ⌐

The sun was creeping toward zenith when she returned to the point of land with a pleasant English-speaking French soldier. He wore no badge of rank on his uniform and had been introduced to her only as "the one who deals with the local people."

"Over there, beyond that bush. You can't see the body from here. It is quite sheltered." She touched his arm and pointed to a spot beyond the bush in full late summer foliage.

She pushed through the undergrowth toward the sparkling water. Ahead of her were the rock and sand, but the soldier was gone.

"We've enough to do without tracking down lost geese." The soldier's words were brusque but there was a twinkle in his eye.

"You mean a wild goose chase?"

"Ah, precisely."

"Why would I have gone to the trouble of finding you if it was not as I told you. I have no interest having you track down lost geese."

He cocked his head and shrugged.

"Look, whoever took him tried to wash his blood off the rock. It pooled in one of the crevasses. You can see where the blood stained the sand. And here where the water from cleaning the rock seeped into the sand."

She wasn't sure why she was pressing her case, when he seemed perfectly willing to go away and leave it alone. It could have nothing to do with his dark hair and amused eyes.

"What were you doing out here?" he asked.

"Looking for a lost sheep."

"Could this not be the blood of your lost sheep?"

"I might think so if I had not seen the soldier's body myself."

He took her by the arm and led her out of the thicket.

"My name is Emile Antony. I will let you know if someone does not return to camp. Good luck finding your sheep."

She watched as he headed away from her back toward the French camp. He had the air of a man who knew where he was going. He glanced up from time to time to watch the clouds gathering over the bay.

When he was out of sight, she turned away to continue her search for the missing ewe.

𝗿 𝗿 𝗿

Joanna was unable to get the sight of the dead soldier out of her mind as she prepared the midday meal for her father and Billy, the hired man. Since her mother had died years ago, these two men were her family. Though Billy was paid scant wages, she thought he stayed with the family out of loyalty, maybe even love. He could have gone to work for almost anyone else for twice the pay. She wondered if her father noticed that she put the best meat, the freshest vegetables, and the largest slice of bread on Billy's plate.

She added thyme and marjoram from the garden to liven up the ordinary ham and onions in butter. She loved the way the odor permeated the room, making it seem more of a feast than something she threw together to cover the fact that she had been gone so long.

"I found the sheep wandering along the creek up by the Hollingsworth house. She had a bit of twine wrapped around her neck." She tossed the improvised halter, braided of horse hair, hemp, and a strip of linen cloth, onto the table in front of her father. She wanted to tell them what else she had found, but each time she tried, the image of the bloody corpse flashed before her eyes. She would tell them after they had eaten.

Her father was more interested in the knife he was sharpening than in anything she might have to say. "I sold two chickens to the Continental army for this." He nudged a few scraps of paper with the tip of the knife. "And a pig to the French for this." He indicated several coins next to the paper.

Joanna slid the money out of the way with her elbow and served the humble meal. Her father offered a prayer of thanksgiving. "Bless the French army with its coins and the Continental army with its scrip, and may they be victorious in Virginia."

Billy, who usually ate in silence, said, "There won't be no food for us this winter if you keep selling it off."

Mr. Clark glared at Billy. "It's not your place to comment on such things. You will be fed well enough."

Joanna smiled to herself at the exchange. She sometimes wondered which of the two men ran the farm. She thought of them as a matched pair, like the oxen that pulled the plow together. Father always won the arguments, but Billy had the last word in how the farm was run. For a brief instant, she felt glad that both men were too old to follow the armies to Virginia. She needed them here.

Joanna was washing the dishes when there was a knock at the door. Her father answered to find a grand and officious French officer standing in the bright midday sunlight. She thought him vain and pretentious just from his bearing and carefully tailored uniform. The odor of some foreign flower wafted off his impeccable white coat with its gold braid. His jewelry, costly metals and polished stone, made her conscious of the poor ornament she wore around her neck, a piece of quartz from the river secured by a thin leather cord.

"I am captain Jules Charbonneau." He spoke his name as though it were a blessing reluctantly bestowed on his listeners. "I will speak to the lady of the house about the business of this morning."

"Joanna?" asked her father.

She stepped out of the interior shadows into the sunlight that was streaming through the door. "While I was out this morning looking for the sheep, I came across a dead French soldier. I sent word to the camp, and when I went to show the body to the soldier, it was gone."

Mr. Clark frowned at his daughter. "You didn't see fit to mention this when you came back from your morning ramble?"

Mr. Clark offered Captain Charbonneau a chair at the plain wood table. Joanna set a candle from the mantel in front of the captain and lit it from the fire with a twig dipped in pine pitch.

"Describe the man, *s'il vous plaît*," the captain demanded.

She tried to keep it simple, but all she could remember was the white coat and the blood.

"Who was the man?" she asked.

"He was a soldier," was the Captain's terse reply.

When Captain Charbonneau was gone, Joanna said to her father, "Do you think the dead man might have been trying to steal our sheep? I found her not far from the body."

Mr. Clark laughed. "The French pay for what they steal. It must have been a Continental. Not a very elegant halter." He held up the improvised twine that she had given him.

🖛 🖛 🖛

Early the next morning, Joanna worked the garden, weeding

and harvesting fresh produce for the day. The late summer weather had encouraged a bounty of food, corn, beans, squash, onions, beets. She would have plenty for her small household with some left over for her friend and neighbor. The ground was damp from the rain that had fallen in the night. The newly risen sun turned the drops on the green leaves to diamonds.

Joanna was shaking the water off the spinach leaves when she saw three men coming down the lane. Captain Charbonneau was as impeccable as he had been the day before. The local constable, in contrast, was disheveled and harried looking. Emile Antony wore the same gentle smile he had bestowed on her yesterday.

Perhaps they were bringing news about the dead soldier.

"Good morning, gentlemen." Joanna wiped her hands on her apron. "What may I do for you?"

"Your hired man, Billy. Where is he?" the constable demanded.

"He should be in the barn." She indicated the rough board structure behind the house. "What do you want with him?"

They turned toward the barn without answering. She knew what they wanted. He was a man of little value, too old for the army, too poor to have political influence. The perfect person to accuse of this murder. No one but the Clarks would care at all.

Joanna chewed a bit of spinach, letting the rich, almost bitter juice trickle down her throat. She smiled as she watched Billy creep out of the back of the barn and head for the woods as his pursuers opened the front door. He must have been watching as they spoke with her. She turned her back to the barn and went on gathering vegetables.

"He is not there. You are hiding him," Captain Charbonneau announced when they had returned to the garden.

She shook her head. "No, I'm not. Why do you want him?" she asked.

"He is suspected of the murder of the French solider you found," Antony explained. "Captain Charbonneau believes that your man caught him trying to steal your sheep and killed him."

"And he brought the body here and then let the sheep go?" she asked.

"You can be sure we will catch him, Miss Clark," the constable said. More, she thought, to appear helpful to the French than to frighten her.

"And then we will have no hired man. You will leave after having eaten us out of house and home and we will starve this winter." She said this to the captain, but meant it for Antony, who seemed more understanding than the others.

"We pay you well enough," said Captain Charbonneau, lifting his chin a hair.

Emile Antony shrugged and shot her an amused smile.

Joanna was surprised to find her friend Mary Chapman in tears when she brought her the vegetables she had harvested.

"Mary, what is it?" Joanna asked as she handed her friend the basket.

"Charles is gone." Mary's usually happy face was gray and haggard as though she had not slept. Her chestnut curls hung limply about her shoulders. Even the sun shining on her bright blue gown failed to cheer the room.

"Charles?"

"Charles Devereaux."

Joanna was silent for a bit, trying to make sense of her friend's misery. "Surely you haven't fallen in love with a French soldier you have known for only a few days."

"He is so handsome, with his black hair and his white uniform. He showed me his ring and told me he is from a prominent family back in France. He said he would take me there, and I would be treated like a princess. He called me Marie. Isn't that beautiful?"

"Ring? What kind of ring?"

"It was a signet ring with his initial carved in it. It was a gray stone that had flecks in it that sparkled gold in the candle light."

Joanna spent a few minutes trying to comfort her foolish friend and then made for the French camp.

She had some trouble making the French-speaking picket understand that she wanted to see Antony.

"It wasn't the stolen sheep," she told him.

"Then what?" He glanced up at a crow calling from a nearby tree.

"You never thought it was, did you? You knew no Frenchman stole the sheep because he wouldn't need to. Nor would he need to make a halter out of scraps of cloth and rope. But a Continental might. Father told me that Billy had overheard two men shouting in French. Father didn't mention it earlier because he didn't want to give you a scrap of information that would send you after Billy again."

Wanting to prove to him she was not as foolish as he must think her, she said, "The dead man's name was Charles Devereaux."

"How did you know?" He turned away from the crow and looked into her eyes.

"I wasn't sure, but it makes sense. I found him close to the house of my friend. He had been courting her. He told her a story about being from a prominent family. Is it true?"

"*Non*, Charles was an orphan who never knew who his parents were."

"He showed her a signet ring to prove it. It belonged to Captain Charbonneau, didn't it?"

"Ah, you are a very observant young woman."

"When I found the body his right arm was extended. I thought he had been reaching for something when he died. Someone might have been pulling a ring off his hand. The 'C' carved in the ring stood for 'Charbonneau' not 'Charles.' Surely French gentlemen do not court local ladies under false pretences and then leave them forever without explanation. Would it not mar Charbonneau's family reputation for the world to think he had such a relative? Captain Charbonneau was trying to get both his reputation and his ring back. He killed your comrade to do it."

"You believe that Captain Charbonneau killed Devereaux to keep his family name clean?"

She nodded. "Later he moved the body so it would look like a local farmer was responsible."

"Can you prove these things?"

"Of course not. I don't much care about the internal conflicts of the French army. I only want to keep Billy from being arrested."

"I will see that he is not arrested. You will need him since we have eaten you out of home and house." His smile lightened the mocking words. "I will take seriously what you have told me. I will look into the matter and share my results with my superior officer. After all, justice is justice, and we cannot have the officers harming the men. It would lead to chaos in the ranks."

Joanna nodded in gratitude. She thought she might miss him after the troops left.

"The idea of falling in love with someone you have known for only a few days," she commented under her breath.

"The very idea," he said as he removed something from his coat pocket and pressed it into her hand.

She was some distance from the French camp when she stopped to look at the note he had given her.

It was a scrap of coarse brown paper with his name, rank, and regiment written in an elegant hand in pencil. Below that he had written, "I will write to tell you the outcome of our investigation. I hope you will see fit to respond when you are able."

KB Inglee works at a Delaware living history museum as an interpreter. This story was born as her site prepared for the March to Victory, a series of events set along Washington's and Rochambeau's route to Yorktown for the final battles of the Revolutionary War. Her historical mystery stories are set in the mid-Atlantic and New England. She has been published in mystery anthologies and on line. She is a past president of Delaware Valley Sisters in Crime.

TROUBLED WATERS

by Peggy Jaegly

"T.J., phone!" Stan Leeper held up the receiver over the heads of their co-workers as if it were the Olympic torch.

"I'm not here!" T.J. Cooper stood with one foot out the door of the Ecology and Oceanographic Office, affectionately nicknamed the Lab.

Stan covered the receiver and shook his head no. "It sounds important. Besides, you're off to your boat for the summer. They won't be able to reach you."

T.J. threw up her hands in defeat and trudged to Stan's desk. "Slave driver!" She stuck her tongue out as she snatched the receiver from him. He grinned and ducked back to the stack of files on his desk.

"Hello?"

"Is this T.J. Cooper?" asked a raspy voice she didn't recognize. "If you want to stay healthy . . ."

"Excuse me, please take me off your call list." T.J. resisted the urge to slam the receiver down. In mock anger, she hit Stan's shoulder with the back of her hand. "You interrupted the start of my scientific research for a sales call!"

"How was I to know?" He looked up at her with concern. "Are you going to be okay? Do you want me to go with you?"

T.J. offered a brave smile to her buddy of many years. "I'll be fine. I have to board the boat sometime. Keep me posted on any developments. I have my cell."

"I will. Call me if you need anything."

T.J. waved goodbye over her shoulder and headed to her car. At home, she flipped through the mail with a cursory glance. She read a handwritten postcard aloud, "You're next." She flipped over the lime green card. No stamp. No return address. "Stupid junk mail! Probably some pizza shop or real estate company with a new-fangled marketing ploy." She tossed the card into her recycling bin.

She surveyed the house. Doors and windows locked. Refrigerator empty and clean. Mail delivery redirected to the dock master at Kent Narrows. Satisfied, she picked up her duffle bag, which was dwarfed by her case of scientific equipment, and loaded them into the car.

An hour later, she pulled into the marina parking lot. As she unloaded her gear, she inhaled the smell of the bay. It never failed to revitalize her . . . or to bring back bittersweet memories of the fun times she shared with her father at the shore.

Overhead, a flying seagull released a mournful cry that echoed the heavy emptiness she felt in her heart. T.J. unsnapped the tarp covering the Bayliner, aptly christened *Happy Ours. This would be her first summer without him. How would she get through this?*

The task of opening up a boat and preparing it for its first voyage since spring distracted her for a couple of hours. Dusk brought a rosy sunset that filled the sky and reached down to caress the water lapping her boat. She heated a can of soup in the galley and set a box of crackers on the table. Only afterwards did she dare to pick up the captain's log, an act she had resisted and avoided since her arrival. Her hand traced the worn binding.

Pain stabbed her heart again. *Maybe if she hadn't. . . .* She clenched her eyes, fighting the tears that wanted to escape whenever she sat still. She studied the photo mounted on the wall of her father hugging her. *What had happened?*

Two years ago, her mother had died in a car accident. Distraught, her father left his position at the Environmental Protection Agency, a job that gave him joy. Now he was missing, presumed dead.

She opened to his last entry. She'd read it a hundred times, searching for any clue. He'd gone out to the stations, especially designated locations for testing for harmful algae and red tides. The same stations where she'd soon be drawing water samples.

Weather: Sunny and calm
Drew samples from the following stations:
10:00 TI Water slightly red
12:00 HI Water clear
15:00 CA Water clear
Cruising to Wye River to investigate reports of possib . . .

His careful printing trailed off, as if he had been interrupted. Then nothing. *How could an experienced boater and fisherman disappear on a fair day?* His body was never recovered, but authorities concluded he drowned.

She closed the log and sighed. "Dad, I know you're here in spirit. If it's the last thing I do, I'm going to continue your work and protect the marshlands from Montgomery's snare. Hopefully my study will convince the planning board to turn down his proposal."

Early the next morning, she downed a cup of black coffee while she tested the engines. Methodically, T.J. completed her mental checklist of boat and safety tasks in preparation for her first ride. With a confident step, she hopped onto the dock and freed the lines. She cleared the side of the boat and climbed the steps to the fly bridge.

I miss you, Dad. Pushing the gears forward she eased her boat out of her slip. A fresh breeze whipped through her short blonde hair. As she listened to the shush-shush of the boat slicing through the waves, her body released some of the tension it had held captive since her father's death. Once out on the open sea, she exhaled a deep breath. *Would life ever return to normal?*

Two hours later Harry, who docked next to her, dropped his cleaning rag to help tie her boat lines to the cleats.

"How was your first ride of the season?"

"The engines are running a little hot. I'm going to take it over to Jack's and have him change the impellers. Don't want to get stuck out there."

Later that day, T.J. cruised over to Jack's Marina at the designated time she'd arranged by phone. She eased her boat into the boat lift and climbed over the hoist to the dock. She signed the work order and instructed Dora, who worked behind the desk, "Have Jack check all the hoses, too. I'm taking some long cruises and everything needs to be in tip top shape."

"We're short-handed today, so it's going to take several hours," Dora warned her. "We'll call you on your cell when it's ready."

T.J. walked a short distance from the marina to a small combination grocery store and deli. Over a sandwich and iced tea, she perused the file she'd brought with her. It contained the latest newspaper articles and promotional material regarding the proposal Nicholas Montgomery had put before the planning board. With the promise of new dollars in the tax bucket, he was pressuring the town to approve his building an elite, gated community. The expense he was downplaying, in her opinion, was the loss of shoreline. Obviously, Montgomery didn't give a second thought to the wildlife, sea life, and flora that lived on that land. With every word she read, she became more determined to stop him.

She checked her watch. She still had time to review her other file. This one contained the details of all the water stations she'd be drawing water samples from to test for toxins. If Montgomery gets his way, she thought, whatever the level is now, it will surely worsen.

Four hours later, her cell phone buzzed with the message that her boat was ready.

"All set, T.J." Jack said. "Your hoses look fine so you shouldn't have any problems. Be careful of grass and seaweed getting caught in the intake, though. Those eel grass strainers I ordered for you haven't come in yet."

"Thanks, Jack," she called as she stepped from the dock to her boat. "I'll be careful."

At her own marina, she had just finished securing her dock lines and placing her fenders when she heard her name called by the dock master.

"Miss T.J.! A letter came for you today."

T.J. wiped her hands on the back of her jeans and reached for it. "Thanks, Pete. I didn't expect to get mail so soon."

"Oh it didn't come in the mail. It was hand delivered." He waited with a look of anticipation. "Some fancy person."

T.J. slid a fingernail underneath the flap of the outer envelope. She glanced up and noticed Pete, who was several inches shorter than her, raise up on his toes, peeking to see what she'd pulled out.

"Really. Thanks again, Pete." T.J. entered the cabin to discourage more conversation. If Pete had his way, he'd want to read the letter and then tell everybody in the marina. She studied the expensive ivory-colored envelope edged in gold. T.J. gasped when she turned the letter over and discovered a gold embossed "M" on the flap. The matching stationery read: "Mr. T.J. Cooper, you are cordially invited to join Nicholas Montgomery for lunch at noon tomorrow at Hemingway's. I wish to present a proposal that will be of great interest to you." The signature was an illegible flourished scrawl. Underneath, the name typed was Nicholas Montgomery.

"Doesn't he know my father is dead?" T.J. asked aloud to no one. She tapped the letter on her open palm. "Rather presumptuous of you, Mr. Montgomery, to assume I'll drop everything to meet you." She tried to ignore the envelope that she tossed in the galley. *This is annoying me*, she admitted to herself an hour later when she realized that her attention kept gravitating to the invitation. *What could he be thinking?*

The next day, despite promising herself that she was going to ignore the letter, five minutes before noon, the maitre d' was leading her to Nicholas Montgomery's table. She'd seen his photo in *Business Today* where he had been touted as "the Golden Boy." Everything he touched turned to money. And beautiful women attached themselves to his arm, if the society page was any indication. T.J. noticed there was a gorgeous brunette sitting with him now, dressed in a low-cut dress more suitable for a nightclub. By comparison, T.J. felt comfortable but dowdy in her taupe dockers and blouse.

"Your party is here, Mr. Montgomery," the maitre d' intoned.

T.J. stepped from behind him and she extended her hand. "Mr. Montgomery."

"You're T.J.?" he asked with obvious surprise as he rose to complete the handshake.

"Were you expecting my father?" she asked.

"Theodore Cooper passed away earlier this year. I was expecting his son."

"No son. I'm T.J."

He turned to his companion who ran her gaze up and down T.J. like an elevator. "Go powder your nose or something, baby."

Without a word to him, nor a backward glance at T.J., she exited.

"Please sit down." Nicholas pulled out a chair opposite him. "Thank you for accepting my invitation."

"Curiosity won over my distaste," she said.

"You're definitely your father's daughter," he acknowledged. "Call me Nick, please." He paused to smile at her. "All my friends do."

"Friends." T. J. let the word hang in the air. *That's probably the charm he uses to meet women.* "Does that mean you've changed your mind about building on the marshlands?"

"Hardly." He chuckled. "But I have a proposal for you that I think you'll accept. Why don't we order first though? I did invite you for lunch."

After they ordered, T.J. asked him, "Did you know my father?"

"We met a few times. I'm sorry for your loss." Nick looked directly at her eyes. "He was a champion for maintaining the bay."

"Yes, he was. I'm picking up where he left off."

During their meal, Nicholas artfully steered the conversation toward asking her what it was like to live on a boat and where to find her favorite cruising spots. She realized during their luncheon why he often met with success. He sincerely listened when others spoke. She also noted that he was evasive. Whenever she asked him a question about himself, somehow the conversation returned to her life.

After refusing dessert but accepting coffee, Nick finally got to the point of their meeting. "Look, T.J., I know you have your pet projects. I'd like to make a trade with you."

"A trade?" T.J.'s body stiffened with resistance.

"I know that you're continuing your father's work. You want to keep the water clean. I can guarantee that my building will not adversely affect what you want." His smile revealed gleaming white teeth that looked great with his tanned skin.

"I don't think you *can* guarantee that, Mr. Montgomery. That would be wishful thinking on both our parts."

"There is, and never has been, any scientific proof that the type of building I do increases bacteria or red tides."

"And there is no proof that it doesn't." The hairs on the back of her neck bristled. "You mentioned a trade?"

"Look, I'm all for your work. I'm a citizen, too. I live here. I want the water to be clean," he assured her. "What I'm proposing is, in return for your public support for my plan at the planning board meeting, I'll be more than happy to fund your independent studies. Further down the coast, you understand."

"You're offering me a bribe?" *Oh, this was too much. What did he take her for?*

"It's not a bribe," he protested. "Consider it a grant. We both know money for your kind of projects is tight."

"This meeting is over, Mr. Montgomery. I'll be at the planning board session," she stood and tossed her napkin on the table, "but it won't be to support anything you're proposing. Thanks for the lunch." She turned and walked fuming out of the restaurant. *The nerve of that guy!*

She had just reached her dock when her cell rang. It was Stan.

"How are things going?" he asked.

"Slow. The boat needed some repairs, but I'm pushing off now. I've got to get and test those water samples for the planning board meeting tomorrow."

"Where are you going?"

She told him her plans.

"Don't forget to go to the one at Hooper Point," he reminded her. "Due to the currents, that area gets hit with the runoff."

"It's on my list."

T.J. turned on her GPS and pulled out her marine charts so she could avoid shallow waters that would strand her boat on sand bars. Her agenda included collecting water samples from Tilghman Island and Hooper Island, where Pfiesteria bacteria had reached Category 3 last year, shutting down the sale of fish, oysters, and crabs, to prevent humans from getting sick from consuming tainted seafood.

At each station, she carefully dipped test tubes, drawing samples of the water. She labeled and replaced the tube in her case for safekeeping. As an added safeguard, on her pocket tape recorder she recorded her findings, both her visual inspections of the water and plant life and her documentation of the GPS coordinates of where she obtained the water samples. She kept her mini-recorder on the voice-activated switch, which kept her hands free for their wet work.

T.J. feared, as her father and other fishermen had, that run-off from Montgomery's proposed community could adversely affect the delicate balance of the water near the marshlands and upset the food chain, which eventually would affect the welfare of humans. If the water proved unsafe now, she had a chance of stopping him. Various environmental groups were trying to stop him, too. If only her study could give them the proof they needed before the damage occurred.

She finished at Hooper Island and decided to take the Eastern Bay route toward Kent Narrows. It would be quicker and less congested with other boaters. She revved up her engines and ran at an angle to the bigger waves. The wind combed through her hair, and she shook her head with delight at the beauty of the ocean.

The sound of another fast approaching boat broke her reverie. It was a big one. A forty-foot Viking. *Didn't they see her? If she didn't know better, they looked like they were heading straight toward her.* She gripped the wheel, readying herself to take evasive action. They were almost upon her, when they cut back their engines and pulled close to her. *Stupid, the waves could knock their boats together.* Their higher deck dwarfed hers. She was surprised when they called her name.

"Yes?" *Who could these men be?*

"We've got a message for you!" a burly man with bulging biceps called to her.

"What's up?" she called back, trying to keep her boat from getting too close to theirs.

"This is what's going to happen to you if you don't keep your nose out of other people's business!" His companions began throwing big, bloody chunks onto her deck and fly bridge. One hit her in the arm. She ducked to avoid one aimed at her head.

"This is your last warning," the leader yelled. "Or you'll end up in the same place as your old man. He didn't listen and look at what happened to him." With that, their engines roared, and they were gone just as quickly as they had arrived.

T.J. gasped and cut her engines back. "Dad?" Her chest constricted and her breath seemed lost. She bent down and picked up one of the chunks. *Shark bait*. She tossed it over the edge. "I've got to get back."

Angry, alarmed, T.J. pushed her throttles forward and headed toward Kent Narrows. *War, they wanted war? They've got it. This just proves that I'm on the right track. I'm getting too close to something someone doesn't want me to know.* She pushed the churning thoughts about her father and his fate down deep inside of her. I'll deal with that later, she consoled herself. *If he died for this, I'm going to see that he didn't die in vain!*

At Crab Alley, she collected her samples quickly but was careful to follow her documentation procedures. As she directed *Happy Ours* toward her marina, she surrendered to an overwhelming urge to check out one of the inlets she was passing. It was near where her father's boat had been found abandoned. She turned the boat around and cut her engines back to a "no wake" speed. She maneuvered the boat as close as possible and threw her anchor out.

Changing into her water suit, and securing her journal and recorder in a waterproof pouch, she jumped into the four feet of water. She didn't have to swim far to be able to wade up to the shore line. *What was she hunting for?* Memories of treks with her father to this area and ones like it tormented her mind. And then she saw a slight movement.

"Well, hello little fellow." She picked up a tiny turtle. "You're really cute! But I don't know what kind you are. Where did you come from?" She had studied all the types of marine life indigenous to this area. This creature matched none.

She documented her find. With a couple of trips back and forth to her boat, she created a makeshift home for the turtle with water and a rock and some food from his habitat.

Once on board, and changed back into dry clothes, she made several calls. They were as excited as she when she described her find. "We've got a meeting tomorrow, my little friend." The turtle gave no indication he understood.

The next day at the planning board meeting, after Nicholas Montgomery made a enthusiastic presentation, complete with drawings, model buildings, and the promise of tax revenues,

T.J. was called to offer her rebuttal.

"Turning that land into a community can't be allowed," she said. After presenting a concise and simplified report on the impact of water runoff to the water and marine life, she announced, "A remarkable discovery was made yesterday." She paused a moment and looked every planning board member in the eye. "I have a witness that will prove that changing the zoning must be stopped. This witness can't speak, so I have brought experts to speak for him."

A murmur ran through the room.

"Who is this witness?" the chairman asked.

From beneath the table, she withdrew the temporary aquarium and placed it in full view. "Him." T.J. looked up at the committee and smiled broadly.

"What is that?" another committeeman asked.

"A turtle."

Laughter howled through the room.

"What does a turtle have to do with these proceedings, Miss Cooper?" The chairman looked disgusted.

"My colleagues can explain that better than I can." Three men rose. She introduced them. "These men are the leading experts in documenting marine life and the viability and possible extinction of species. They will testify that this is a new type of turtle, unknown until now. Since it's a previously undiscovered species, the law prevents the land from being touched."

After the scientists offered their testimonies and confirmed T.J.'s claim, the committee moved to turn the matter over to their legal consultant for his interpretation.

Out in the hallway, Nick Montgomery approached her with a smile. "Not bad, T.J. You won."

T.J. ignored the hand he proffered. "There is still the matter of the warning I received yesterday, Mr. Montgomery. I will be pursing justice in that arena as well."

He looked puzzled. "What are you referring to?"

"As if you didn't know." She walked away. Her last-minute preparations for this meeting hadn't left any time to make a report about yesterday to anyone.

Stan came up to her. "Congratulations, you did it!"

"All the credit goes to this little fellow." T. J. glanced gratefully at the turtle who lay still, oblivious to what he had accomplished. "I'm off to take him to the Institute. They'll study him before returning him home."

When T.J. reached her car, another surprise awaited her. The front seat was covered in dead fish. She picked up a slip of paper. *Another message?* She felt the blood drain from her face when she read the scrawl. *You'll be joining them in the deep blue sea.*

The smell overwhelmed her. After carefully securing a safe spot for her turtle, she retrieved a garbage bag and gloves from her trunk and placed the fish into it. A slippery and distasteful job.

Stan cruised by her car in the parking lot and stopped. Through an open window he called, "Are you having car trouble?"

"It's trouble all right."

"Whew!" Stan tried to wave the stink away. "Who did this?"

"I don't know. Somebody who doesn't like losing." He helped her clean out her car. Then, she threw the bag and gloves into a nearby trash can.

"Stan, listen. I don't have time to either wait for an officer or go to the police station. I have to take care of this precious turtle. Would you do me a favor?"

"What do you need?" he asked.

"Since the police are right here, and you've seen this mess, will you go and report it and ask them to meet me on the boat later? Take them this note. I'm tired and I have some other things to tell them, too."

"Sure thing. Guess whoever did this should know by now that you're not going to be stopped by a little bait."

"Thanks, you're a real friend," she said, relieved.

T.J. drove her new little friend to his temporary quarters where he'd be photographed and observed by qualified and caring scientists. On her way to back to her boat, something niggled at the edge of her consciousness but she couldn't quite grasp the thought trying to emerge. I'm just exhausted, she thought.

She gathered her purse and briefcase and slipped her recorder back into her pocket, where it felt familiar. As she walked through the parking lot, she observed a fisherman changing his day's catch from a smaller cooler to a larger one by his car. *Fish.* The image brought back this morning's warning and the smell that still clung to her car seat and carpets . . . and, something else. Something Stan had said.

She stopped abruptly. He had said that the bait couldn't stop her. Bait. Fish. She hadn't told anyone yet about the incident. She had been busy lining up the reinforcements for the planning board presentation. So, the only way he could know was . . . she checked her watch. It had been two hours since she left him. T.J. dialed the police station on her phone. When the dispatcher answered, she asked, "My friend Stan Leeper and I needed to file a report on vandalism. Has he been in to make the report?"

The voice on the other end checked, then answered in the negative. "Do you want to speak to an officer now?"

"No, I'll come in later myself," and she cut the connection before the dispatcher could ask any more questions.

T.J. decided to drop her things at the boat and change out of the heels she rarely wore and exchange her business suit for a comfortable outfit. Then, she'd go to the police herself.

"Hi ya, T.J.!" Harry hailed her from his tuna tower. "How'd it go?"

"Great! I think we're going to win after all!" She smiled broadly and waved.

She went below to her cabin, tossed her briefcase on the bed, opened the door to her tiny closet, and peered in to select a comfortable outfit. There wasn't much light below, and the contents of her minute storage area were illuminated by the daylight that managed to creep in from a small window at the back of the boat. Just as she reached in to grab a pair of slacks, a dark shadow fell over her. Turning quickly, she saw Stan looming over the small opening at the top of the steps. He blocked her only means of escape. "T.J."

"Y-y-yes?" She hated the quaver in her voice. She mustn't tip him that she knew he was involved in something sinister. "Good of you to drop by. How'd it go at the station?"

"Fine. Officer Murphy wrote up a report," he claimed. "Unfortunately, with no witnesses, there isn't much they can do. Guess you're out of luck."

"Is that so? Uh, I was going to change, if you'd excuse me a minute." She felt for her cell from the outside of the pocket. If she could just get him to give her five minutes, so that she could call for help.

"No need." He descended two steps, enough to show her the gun he held. "You and me are going for a ride. Let's go."

T.J., her mind feverishly looking for an escape, climbed the steps. Stan followed her out to the deck. He shoved the gun into his pocket, but she knew it was trained on her.

"No false moves," he warned her. "You smile pretty, and act like I'm an old friend and we're going for a quick ride. Of course, it will be your last."

T.J.'s mind whirled. She climbed the ladder to the captain's station. It wasn't easy in slippery heels.

"Going for a ride?" Harry called to her.

"You bet," T.J. forced a smile. "Can't miss this great weather."

She saw Harry look at her funny, but turned to start the engines. She didn't want anything bad to happen to Harry. Best to do what Stan wanted.

The canal to the bay was a posted no wake zone. She could steer easily and talk to Stan. "Stan, we've been friends for a long time. What's this about?"

"It's about you sticking your nose too far into other people's business."

"Whose?"

"Doesn't matter," Stan's face contorted in anger. "You just don't know when to stop."

"Stop what?"

"Saving the fish, saving the water. You name it."

"Stan, we *both* work for the Lab. That's what we do!" she said.

"That's what *you* do, not me. I'm smarter than that." Stan smiled sardonically. "You're . . . just like your father. He didn't believe the warnings either. He paid a *big* price for not taking his warnings seriously." He laughed maniacally. "So did your mother."

The boat was approaching the end of the canal. Now, she had to navigate around the markers, still going slow. T.J. knew she needed an immediate plan. Pretending to sniff and rub her eyes, she feigned reaching into her pockets, as if searching for a tissue. With one hand, she hit the redial button. Her phone was still on mute from the meeting. She turned the dial volume down, so that whoever answered wouldn't be heard. With her other hand she flipped the on switch of her tape recorder.

"My m-m-mother. She died in a car accident."

Stan looked satisfied and proud. "It wasn't an accident."

T.J. gasped as the full impact of Stan's words. Her mother had been *murdered*!

"You killed my mother?"

"Your father ignored the warnings. He was stubborn, but you are dense." He sneered. "You thought the phone call I arranged was a sales call. You ignored the warning left in your mailbox. Your mother was collateral damage in convincing your father. You're going to pay for your stupidity."

"How dare you!" Rage surged in T.J., and she lunged at Stan. "You killed an innocent human being. My mother. She didn't deserve that!"

"Watch it! Steer the boat." His hand, still in his pocket, thrust forward, reminding her she was literally under the gun.

"What about my father?" Her abhorrence and her tears made seeing the markers and steering difficult.

"I jet-skied out to his boat. He thought I had come to help collect samples. He never knew until the last minute that I worked for the developers he was trying to thwart."

"H-h-how did he die?"

"I stabbed him, then threw him overboard."

"I had an argument with him that day," T.J. croaked. "I never got a chance to apologize." Tears streamed down her cheeks. "Do you work for Montgomery?"

"That moron." Stan snorted. "There are others with bigger fish to fry. Montgomery was too short-sighted to see the benefits."

He laughed at his own joke, which T. J. didn't find funny.

She wanted to reach out and throttle that laugh and squeeze it out of his throat. She gripped the steering wheel with a fierce determination. *He was not going to escape his due.* Despite the challenges, she had cleared the channel markers.

"Open her up!" Stan ordered her.

T. J. pushed full throttle. When they had raced out several miles, beyond where any other boaters were visible, he told her to cut the engines. She complied and turned and glared into his face. "What's in this for you?"

"Money, lots of it! I'm a well-paid mole for big developers. Easy money," he bragged. "I work for the opposition and pass along the plans, the studies being done, and sometimes even alter studies to suit their purposes. I give them what they want. I get paid. Sweet."

"In other words, you're a sell-out, Stan." An unexpected calm enveloped her. Anger made her numb to the danger. Even if she died, she refused to go without a fight. With no witnesses, Stan had pulled the gun into view. He brandished it and signaled her to go down the steps. Just as she reached the edge of the first step, she turned, as all boaters do, to face the steps they climb or descend. Instead of stepping down, she lunged forward, grabbing the wrist of his gun-toting arm. He fell backward and she on top of him. They were struggling for control when she heard a thundering roar and wondered if that's how everyone's blood sounded just before they were going to die.

"Drop your weapon, you're surrounded!" a voice cried from the sky.

Turbulent wind surrounded them as a helicopter descended and SWAT team members jumped on board. They quickly subdued Stan and disarmed him. Within minutes, harbor patrol boats corralled their boat.

As they handcuffed him, T.J., still laying on the deck breathless, asked hoarsely, "How did you know?"

"Your dock neighbor reported a possible abduction."

"How did he know?"

"He insisted that you had to have been kidnapped because you would *never* go boating in heels. Said you were too much of a tomboy to do that fool thing. Then when headquarters got your call, we heard what was going on."

"Oh, here," T.J. reached into her pocket. "I got it all on tape."

"Brilliant." The captain beamed.

🐾 🐾 🐾

A few weeks later, Nicholas Montgomery came to her table.

"Thanks for the invite," he said. "I was happy to hear from you."

"It's the least I could do. I kind of feel like I owe you an apology."

"No need. I've read about what happened in the papers. Sorry." He stared sincerely into her eyes. "I heard the good news though. They're naming the turtle after your father."

"Well, he deserves it for what he suffered. The new species will be called the 'Teddy Cooper.' It will be a lasting memorial to him to immortalize his work for the area."

"He earned the honor." Nicholas agreed.

"I asked you here to present a proposal of my own," T.J. admitted.

"That sounds intriguing."

"Would you be interested in a way to make money off the land you own *and* maintain the ecology?"

"I'm all ears." He flashed a smile, encouraging her to continue.

"I thought it would be great if an outdoor nature park was created. You could call it something like 'Montgomery's Marine Sanctuary.' It would be like the African safari parks, where people stay in their cars or special vehicles and the wildlife runs free. On the one patch of land, you could build a hands-on educational nature center and give guided tours and lectures and sell souvenirs."

"It has possibilities," Nicholas stroked his jaw thoughtfully. "But you'd have to prove how profitable an investment it would be for me."

"I understand." She handed him a portfolio. "This contains the full proposal, including the expenditures and expected revenue."

"I'll have my people look it over." Nick smiled at her. "I like your style, T.J. If we accept this proposal, would you be willing to help draw up the plans as a representative of the Ecology and Oceanographic Office?"

"It would be my pleasure," T.J. answered. "Anything to preserve the bay."

"Of course, this may require many meetings, long meetings, to convince me about this project."

"You're ever the charmer, Nick. Don't think I'm going to back down on anything when it comes to keeping the water clean and the wildlife healthy."

"I expect no less." Nick grinned. "Perhaps we could begin negotiations over a candlelit dinner?"

T.J. paused then smiled. "Only if they don't serve turtle soup."

Peggy Jaegly is a professional harpist who entertains herself by thinking up mystery plots. While the characters and events depicted are fictional, the boat *Happy Ours* does cruise the Chesapeake Bay. If you happen to spot it, you're invited aboard to say hello to the captain and his first mate. Read more of her mysteries in *Crime Scene: NJ* and *Who Died In Here?* Learn more by visiting her website, www.peggyjaegly.com.

BEEDE AND THE BAREFOOT BODY

by Clyde Linsley

December, 1833

"Well, Mr. Beede, how about it?" said the captain of the watch. He pronounced the name in two syllables — Bee-dee — as many Southerners did, despite several years' acquaintance. "Do you recognize this man or not?"

Josiah Beede leaned over the body and held the lantern close to the face. It was a young man, he could see, with dark hair plastered to his face, uncovering one brown, staring eye. The face was badly battered, not surprisingly; a passage through the Great Falls of the Potomac would have that effect, even on a dead man. The Potomac River at Washington City was rapidly freezing over, but Beede suspected the river never froze completely here at the rapids.

"His name is Arthur Gould," Beede said. "I met him only yesterday. He sought an interview with President Jackson concerning some federal lands."

"The president is not in the city," the watch captain said.

"Which is precisely what I told him," Beede replied. "Mr. Gould was most unhappy about that. He left my office, and I did not see him again."

"What time was this?"

"I don't recall precisely. Perhaps half past three o'clock. Perhaps a bit later."

"He had this in his pocket," the watch captain said. He handed Beede a slip of paper. Upon perusal, Beede saw that he held an unpaid bill from Brown's Indian Queen Hotel, on which someone had written Beede's name and office address.

"Who found him?" Beede asked.

"A local farmer," the watch captain said. "But he couldn't have been responsible for this man's death. That must have occurred farther upstream."

"He'd hardly have reported it if he had been responsible,"

Beede agreed.

The dead man wore a black frock coat of high quality and trousers made of good serge material. His hat, if he had had one, must have been lost downstream, and his feet were bare. Could the raging waters have taken his boots as well as his hat? Beede thought it unlikely, but stranger things had happened.

"Why did Mr. Gould want to see the president?" the watch captain asked.

"He didn't tell me," Beede said. "Since the president wasn't around, I didn't bother to ask further."

"Most unusual," the watch captain said. "I can't imagine what he was doing so far from the city. Few men come here late at night except for nefarious purposes."

🟊 🟊 🟊

The knock at Beede's door had come in the early morning hours, awakening his wife, Adrienne, who desperately needed her rest, for she was in the final stages of a difficult pregnancy. The child slave Dicey had brought the news that a night watchman was at the door asking for him. Beede had acquired some reputation as a crime solver in his time in Washington, so he was not entirely surprised. It was also common knowledge in Washington City that he held an important, if unofficial, position in President Jackson's "kitchen cabinet."

Randolph joined him downstairs. Beede had come to depend on the younger man's intelligence and judgment. Never mind that he was a slave, like Dicey, and belonged to Adrienne, not to him. In the Beede household, Randolph was nominally a butler, which was an inessential function in such a small household, but Beede relied on him increasingly as a sounding board and advisor. Beede would have freed him if he could, but it was becoming increasingly difficult to free slaves, in Washington City or anywhere else in the South. The law discouraged manumission and required any freed slave to leave the District of Columbia. Similar laws prevailed elsewhere.

"They sent Gilroy this time," Randolph said as he accompanied Beede to the front room where the watchman stood waiting nervously. "The captain must think this a serious matter to send his most experienced man."

"Did he give you any idea of the nature of the problem?"

"Only that they have found a body."

"I'd like for you to accompany me. You have good instincts in these matters."

"The captain may object. Or Gilroy."

"Let him object. I need your eyes and your mind."

⌐ ⌐ ⌐

If the watchman objected to the colored man's company, he had shown no sign of it during the long carriage ride out of the city to the place where the Potomac River frothed over the fall line in fury.

⌐ ⌐ ⌐

"We found this feller washed up on the river bank," Gilroy the watchman said to Beede as the three men rode toward the falls. "He was beat up pretty bad, probably by the river. We're hoping you can put a name to him."

"What makes you think I'll have more success at that than you will?" Beede asked.

"You'll see when we get there."

Washington, D.C., had been built at nearly the head of navigation on the Potomac River. Although efforts to extend the river by canal were continuing, it was turning out to be a more costly and difficult undertaking than anyone had anticipated. Beede wondered if it would ever be completed, and he was not alone in this. Construction of the locks and dams that were needed in order to skirt the falls had been a major obstacle, and the terrain grew even more rugged as the canal progressed westward.

The Great Falls had been responsible for more than one death in the years Beede had lived in Washington City. Most of its victims had been citizens on Sunday carriage rides, whose curiosity had led them too close to the furious waters. One misstep could easily end a life.

They heard the falls long before they saw them, a soft thunder that grew steadily louder as they approached. Eventually they saw the river's phosphorescent glow as it plunged through the cataract on its way to the Chesapeake Bay. The watch captain stood on the near shore, awaiting them.

"Thank you for coming, Mr. Beede," he had said. "I'm afraid we have a nasty one for you."

Afterward, as they rode back to the city, Beede and Randolph conferred about what they had seen.

"Was it an accident?" Randolph said. "The Great Falls are treacherous. If you fall in, you'll probably drown before you could make it to the riverbank, especially in this winter weather."

"I don't think it was an accident," Beede said. "Why would the victim come all this distance alone except to meet someone in secret? And if such a meeting took place, why shouldn't the person he met try to save him? I think he was murdered."

"He had hardly been in town long enough to make enemies," Randolph said.

"Perhaps not," Beede said. "But let us see what we can learn."

More than most cities its size, Washington had many alleys. Its crazy-quilt streets cut this way and that, carving city blocks into odd shapes and creating narrow back passageways, where slave and freedman lived side by side. It was into this milieu that Randolph entered the next evening in search of a hack driver about whom he had learned from discreet inquiries among the staff at the Indian Queen Hotel.

"I remembers the man, all right," the cabbie said. "I picked him up at the hotel about sunset. Couldn't think why he'd want to go out to the Great Falls so late. Not much to see there after dark, and it's a long way to travel."

"Was he meeting someone, do you think?"

"Must've been, but there weren't nobody else around when we got there. Leastwise nobody I saw. I just left him off, like he tol' me, and drove back to town."

"Did he say anything to you on the way out there? Why he was going? What he was going to do there? Anything like that?"

"White folks don't talk much to colored," the cabbie said. "A lot of the time they don't even notice we're there."

▅ ▅ ▅

Beede, meanwhile, went to the hotel and talked to the clerk at the desk. Gould had registered two days before, the clerk said, and had asked immediately how to find Beede's law offices. The ledger, signed with Gould's immaculate signature, indicated that he lived in Cincinnati.

"Strange. I know no one in Cincinnati," Beede said.

"Cincinnati's a growing community," the clerk said. "You might be surprised. People are pouring in every day. Most of them don't stay, of course; they catch a riverboat down the Ohio to the western lands. You probably know a number of people in Cincinnati — without realizing it. Besides, your reputation precedes you."

"Perhaps," Beede said, doubtfully. "Did he say anything else to you?"

"He asked about the whereabouts of the slave markets," the clerk said. "'There's one right across the street,' I told him. 'You can't miss it.'"

The slave markets were among Beede's least favorite places in Washington. As a New Englander, he found slavery shameful. He despised his own guilty involvement in what southerners were fond of calling the "peculiar institution."

The existence of not one, but several, bustling slave markets in the nation's capital city was particularly distasteful, he thought, but he was in no position to object. He was married to a southern woman, who owned slaves and had brought slaves to the marriage as part of her dowry. He lived in a city in which slavery was not only legal but extremely popular.

Swallowing his disgust, Beede visited each of the dealers in turn, beginning with those closest to the hotel.

"I remember him," said the first slave dealer he questioned. "He was looking for a boy about sixteen years old. I had a couple on hand, but neither seemed to suit him."

"Did he buy a slave, then?"

"Not from me," the dealer said. "And not from any other dealer, I'll wager. My stock is the best in town."

A canvass of other dealers confirmed that Gould had visited each dealer in turn but had left each establishment without making a purchase. In most instances, the exchange had taken only a few minutes. After looking quickly over the slaves on hand, Gould would walk away.

"It was as if he had someone particular in mind," one dealer said. "Maybe he saw a slave somewhere that struck his fancy, and he was trying to find him again."

"He was from Cincinnati," Beede said, puzzled. "Ohio is a free state, I had thought."

"From the very first day," the dealer confirmed. "Still, that ain't my worry, is it, if he wants to smuggle a slave back home to a free state? I'll get my money either way."

▄ ▄ ▄

"Why do you concern yourself with the death of this man?" Adrienne asked him that evening. "His death may be unfortunate, but it's nothing to do with you. You have a responsibility to your law practice."

"I've little confidence in the abilities of the night watch," Beede replied. "If Washington had a proper police force, like New Orleans or some other big city, I could perhaps feel justified in leaving the matter in their hands, but our night watch is not prepared to deal with the exploration of criminal motives and evidence, while I have had some experience in this area."

"Does it matter?" she said. "You need not shoulder all the problems of the world. You undertake too much."

"Justice matters," Beede said. "I am a lawyer. I cannot look away when injustices occur. It is a violation of my oath."

"And your marriage vows? You promised to keep and protect me. Are you not concerned with my health, and with the health of our child? What would I do if you are far away when I am in need of you?"

"I have not violated my vows, and I would not," he said. "But I have other responsibilities, as well, and I must see to them."

▄ ▄ ▄

The following day, Beede returned to the Indian Queen Hotel and asked to inspect Gould's room.

"That room has been rented," the hotel clerk said. "I can't leave a room vacant; that's bad business. And we've removed all of Mr. Gould's possessions, in any case."

"Where are his possessions, then? I may not need to visit the room if I can see them."

The clerk led Beede to a storeroom where a small carpetbag sat forlornly against a wall.

"That is all he had with him," the clerk said. "You may take it with you. I've no need of it, and I have no address to send it to."

The bag yielded little: a receipt from a local boot maker for a pair of Hessian boots, a razor and leather strap, a shaving brush, a clean shirt, a Bible. Beede had expected to find more, but he wrote a list of everything and stuffed it in his pocket. He took the bag and its contents, as well, and went in search of the boot maker.

The boot maker's shop was only three blocks from the Capitol building, but it stood essentially in a wilderness. More than 30 years after President John Adams had moved the national government to this location, the city — if city it was — remained isolated and largely deserted for nearly ten months of the year. The arrival of the Congress annually filled the local boardinghouses to overflowing, but few people lived here year-round. Most preferred to return to their home districts as soon as possible after the legislature adjourned. Even President Jackson found it possible to return home for an extended visit or two.

The boot maker remembered Gould.

"He was quite pleased with his order," the man said. "They're as fine a pair of boots as ever I made. They were black leather with tassels at the vee-cut. I remember because many customers ask me to leave off the tassels, but Mr. Gould was quite insistent. Did he recommend me to you?"

"Mr. Gould is dead," Beede said. "His body washed up on the riverbank below the Great Falls."

"Tragic, indeed. But how can I help you?"

"I'm attempting to determine where he might have gone

after leaving your establishment," Beede said.

"Perhaps I *can* help you, there," the boot maker said. "He asked for directions before he left. He was looking for the Jenkins plantation. It's over toward Aldie, in Virginia."

"That's quite a long way to go."

"He said he was looking for a slave," the boot maker said. "I was given to understand it was a particular slave he had in mind, and that he was on the Jenkins property."

▗ ▗ ▗

Beede left his house early the following morning to rent a horse for the ride to the Jenkins plantation. It was a long trip, taking him from the Potomac River valley into the foothills of the Shenandoah Mountains. The road grew steeper, and the hills rockier, the farther he traveled. He arrived at the plantation in mid-afternoon and tied off his horse to a tree in the front of the house. It was a ramshackle dwelling place, in desperate need of a coat of whitewash and, perhaps, some roof repairs.

A man appeared in the doorway, a tall, weather-beaten man dressed in threadbare homespun, with wiry gray hair and a prominent mouth.

"He'p you?"

"Perhaps," Beede said. "I'm attempting to trace the movements of a gentleman who arrived at Washington City earlier in the week. His name is Arthur Gould. He was a dark-haired man in, I would guess, his early twenties. About my height, I would say."

"Never heard of him."

"Perhaps he didn't use his name," Beede said. "Anybody who looks like that come around?"

"Wouldn't matter what name he used. Ain't had no visitors at all for near onto a month."

"Nobody looking to buy a slave?"

"Nope. Ain't got but two, and I ain't selling. I need the he'p. I ain't one of them Tidewater gentleman planters with their thousand-acre farms. It's just me and two darkies. I jist grow a acre or two of corn to eat and a little tobacco, for the cash money."

A wasted trip, then. Beede thanked the man for his time

and turned his horse to go, but as he rode away, he glimpsed a figure peeking from around the corner of the house. The man was signaling to him.

Beede glanced behind him. The man in the doorway — Jenkins, he supposed — had gone back inside the house. Beede rode slowly up to the man who gestured to him.

"You lookin' for Mistah Gould?" the man said. He was dark as a walnut, with a prominent nose. Beede assumed he was one of Jenkins's two slaves.

"Mr. Gould is dead," Beede replied.

"Not *that* Mr. Gould," the man said. "T'other one. The brother."

"I know nothing of a brother," Beede said.

The man seemed confused. "Why'd you come out here, then? You from Washington City, ain't you?"

"That's right."

"Well, Mistah Gould's brother is here. Ain't he the one you lookin' for?"

"I was unaware that he had a brother."

"Oh, he got a brother, all right. He's a slave like me."

"Can you take me to him?"

"Not now, I can't. Massah Jenkins will see me. You needs to come back after dark," the man said.

Beede thought about his situation. Was there any point in returning after dark? It was a long ride back to Washington City, and he would be hard-pressed to reach it before he lost the daylight. Adrienne would be upset as it was; she was emotionally fragile at present with a baby on the way. He should not burden her with new uncertainties at this time.

"I'll return *tomorrow* night," he said. "Where shall we meet?"

┏ ┏ ┏

"If Mr. Gould's brother is a slave," Randolph said that evening, "why was not Mr. Gould a slave, also?" He sat with Beede in the parlor of Beede's house after Adrienne had gone to bed.

"I don't know," said Beede. "Slave status passes down through the mother, as you know. Perhaps they're only half brothers, and Arthur Gould's mother was free."

"He could also have been *given* his freedom, or purchased it," Randolph said. "He lived in Ohio, you said? Many freed slaves have moved to Ohio."

"That's possible, I suppose."

"Or perhaps," Randolph said, after a moment's thought, "Arthur Gould's brother was also free before he was abducted."

"Captured and forced into slavery, you mean?" Beede said. "That's possible, too. The demand for slaves has been growing rapidly since it became illegal to import them from abroad. Of course, forcing a free man into slavery is a criminal offense."

"If Mr. Gould had evidence that his brother was a free man, that would be a strong motive for someone to murder him," Randolph pointed out.

"And unfortunately," Beede said, "the courts would tend to favor a free white man in any dispute of this nature. Mr. Gould's brother would not even be permitted to testify in his own behalf."

That evening, in frustration, Beede once again pored over the meager possessions that Arthur Gould had brought with him. The boot maker's receipt was self-explanatory, he thought, but it proved only that Arthur Gould had purchased a pair of boots. The shirt was only a shirt; the razor and strap and brush were merely what they appeared to be.

Then he began leafing through the Bible. The book contained, in addition to Scripture, the usual family tree information on the flyleaf. Gould's name was there; Beede studied it carefully. As he had surmised, Gould did, indeed, have a brother who was six years younger.

The entries went back only three generations, and only the two most recent entries had been made in Cincinnati. The earliest entry, made around the time of the Revolutionary War, had been added in Georgia. It occurred to Beede that this was the hallmark of the descendants of freedmen; three generations previously they had probably been slaves. Beede wondered whether they had been manumitted, had purchased their freedom, or had escaped. It was not unusual for people of color to obtain their freedom by one means or another, nor was it unusual for them to pass for white.

When freedmen acquired some wealth, often they attempted to buy freedom for other family members. The slave dealers who remembered Gould had said he seemed to be searching for a particular person. Perhaps he was seeking to buy freedom for his brother.

It was indicative, but not definitive, Beede thought. He needed something more in order to move forward in the direction his mind was pointing out to him.

◤ ◤ ◤

"Arthur is dead?" the young man said when they met the following evening, and Beede could hear the consternation in his voice. "Then I am lost. He was my only hope."

"So you knew him. Were you related?"

"He was my brother — half brother. His mother was white, and free. Mine was a mulatto slave. We grew up together until my father sold me."

The young man, who said his name was Thomas, was hardly darker in complexion than his brother, Beede thought, and might easily, in different circumstances, have passed for white. They had met in a hickory grove far from the farmhouse, not long after dark. Thomas Gould had arrived in the company of the slave who had spoken to Beede the previous day, and who had quickly disappeared.

"Your own father sold you?"

The young man favored him with a wry smile. "I believe he loved me, in his fashion, but he needed money."

Beede could imagine it, for he had seen it before. To some slaveholders, their slave offspring were considered merely another cash crop. Some, in fact, encouraged procreation among their slaves in order to acquire a ready source of income, and many were more than willing to provide for themselves the seed that made their slaves fruitful.

"Before I was taken away, Arthur came to me and said he would redeem me as soon as he could," Thomas Gould said. "That was two years ago; I suppose it has taken him this long to raise the necessary funds. And now, you tell me, he is dead, and I am truly lost."

"Perhaps not," Beede said. "I do not wish to raise false hopes, but I have an idea that may be helpful."

r r r

Early the following week, Beede heard someone knocking on the door to his office. He opened the door to find a man standing there, the gray man from the Jenkins plantation.

"Your name Beede?" the man said.

Beede nodded assent, and the man entered. "You sent me this note that says you got a surprise for me? Something I should dress up for?"

"Yes, I did," Beede said. "Come with me to the other room, where we can discuss the matter further."

He escorted the man into the inner office, where another man sat waiting expectantly.

"We reading a will or somethin'?" Jenkins asked, seeing the seated man.

"Not precisely," Beede said, "Although we are concerned with the deceased."

He glanced at the other man, who nodded.

"Those are the boots I made for Arthur Gould," he said. "I'd recognize them anywhere."

Beede dismissed the boot maker, who left the room, and turned to Jenkins.

"That gentleman is a boot maker in this city," Beede told Jenkins. "He made a fine pair of boots for a visitor. His customer picked up the boots last week. No doubt you see the problem," he added.

"I do not," said Jenkins. "Many boots look alike, and Hessians are quite in fashion nowadays."

"It should not be so very difficult to show that these are the same boots that were made for Arthur Gould, who was found barefoot when his body washed up on the river bank. The boot maker has his lasts, after all."

"All right, Mr. Beede, you're correct. Gould came to visit me last week, wearing these boots, and I admired them so much that he gave them to me. Very generous of him, I'd say."

"Boots that he had purchased only hours earlier? I think not. I doubt that the captain of the watch will believe that story, either. I believe Mr. Gould came to you with the intention of purchasing his brother's freedom, but you refused to sell. And in the dispute that followed, you killed him."

Jenkins considered this for a moment and sighed.

"What is it that you want of me, Beede?" he said. "If you intended to arrest me, you would have had the watch captain waiting for me here. Since you did not, I assume you have something else in mind."

"That is correct."

"So what is it that you want from me?"

"I want your slaves," Beede said.

▰ ▰ ▰

"I don't understand why it was necessary for Jenkins to come to your office," Randolph said that evening.

"I thought Jenkins would probably dress up to come into the city," Beede said, "and he wouldn't resist the opportunity to wear his new boots. I needed to see those boots in order to make my case against him."

"Do you regret anything about this affair?" Randolph asked Beede. "After all, Jenkins has gone free, despite his murderous act."

"I *do* regret that," Beede admitted. "However, I could not be certain that Jenkins would be convicted of his crime, given the predilection of southern juries to give the benefit of the doubt to slaveholders. This way, at least, Mr. Gould's brother is free and on his way back to Ohio, along with his fellow slave."

"Jenkins will simply acquire another slave," Randolph said.

"No doubt," Beede said. "But two slaves have been freed, and that is a not inconsiderable accomplishment."

<hr />

Clyde Linsley is the author of three historical mystery novels featuring nineteenth century New England sleuth Josiah Beede. "Beede and the Barefoot Body" takes place in 1833, prior to the three Josiah Beede novels, when Beede is living in Washington and serving in Andrew Jackson's unofficial "kitchen cabinet." Clyde lives in Washington's Northern Virginia suburbs with his wife and a significant number of debts.

BACKSEAT

by C. Ellett Logan

Raleigh Prentiss, drunk and diminutive, leaned against the closed bathroom door at her sister-in-law's house and practiced her invisibility, letting the melodious sound of tinkling glasses and the grinding churn of the garbage disposal wash over her. The party's kitchen-music was punctuated by the staccato of the front door closing as other guests, sometimes in groups, and sometimes one couple at a time, called it a night. Eventually, she entered an empty hallway and followed the people-sounds to her husband who stood on a deck off the family room, in a small knot of smokers, laughing too loudly and too long at someone's joke. Guy caught sight of his wife and moved his beefy frame around the outside of the group without interrupting the next smoker's story, brushing past her and out the front door, leaving Raleigh to thank the hosts.

A streetlight, with its spiky halo of humidity, illuminated the driveway as she made her way to the car and climbed into the passenger seat. The cacophony of the summer night, bellowing frogs, and screeching insects, scarcely penetrated her alcohol-induced dullness. At last they were on their way home, neither in any condition to drive. They attempted to follow the MapQuest printout directions in reverse but still managed to miss the exit to I-64. In frustrated silence the couple crisscrossed Tidewater back country roads for more than thirty minutes. Raleigh knew from the grim set of her husband's jaw that she would not make it home without catching hell. Guy's reservoir of fury ran deep. The alcohol that they had consumed at the party magnified his illusion of sanctimonious superiority and blunted her ability to defend herself. Resigned and weary, she tucked her thin legs up under her body and stared at her ghostly reflection in the car's side window.

Guy punched in the lighter and groped the front of his black knit shirt, working a pack of cigarettes out of its pocket. Taking both hands off the wheel he brought the lighter toward his face, and for a moment in the warm red glow of the lit cigarette, Raleigh saw the hint of a smile. He took a deep drag then veered sharply off the bumpy band of gravel road they had mistakenly turned onto and down a dirt lane bordered by a tangle of kudzu-smothered trees and underbrush.

"Stop this!" Raleigh pleaded. "We're lost!" She grabbed for the seatbelt she had neglected to buckle as the car fishtailed violently, pitching her against the dashboard, then down onto the floorboards, unleashing a stream of swearwords from her normally reticent mouth. Finally Guy pumped the brakes, fighting for control as the vehicle lurched over several deep ruts and stopped. Raleigh wrenched open the door and scrambled out into the moist, pre-dawn air.

Guy looked straight ahead. "Get back in the car, Leigh." His tone was cold and measured.

Raleigh, very tired, nudged her door shut with her foot, then backed away from the car. She stumbled a few steps down the pitted road. Guy gunned the engine and swung the car around, its spinning tires kicking up clods of mud that narrowly missed her head. She had just taken the bravest, most important steps of her life. There was no going back now. Raleigh watched with relief as Guy's taillights blurred into distant red novas and vanished. She continued on toward the pastel light of the dawn as it squirted from the horizon.

r r r

Mercer Tibodeau was as sinewy as rawhide shoelaces after a lifetime working on his wife's family estate. He hunched over the prissy sink in the powder room off the foyer, splashing water onto the gray stubble of his face and crew cut. His pink, scrawny wife, Claire, shoved the door open.

"Didn't you hear me calling you from the garage?" she asked, pushing him aside to look at herself in the mirror.

Tibodeau remained silent.

"If I can get up before dawn to get things ready," she continued, "couldn't you at least get the God damned cases of wine out of the car? I want to start prepping for the party before I go to church." She fluffed her bangs. "Everyone's coming at four," she barked, then marched down the hall to the kitchen.

Tibodeau went back to running water, rinsing the sink to purge the orange-scented soap he'd dispensed, sorry that he *could* understand what she was yelling — even from the other end of the long hall.

"So. I bet you're going to pout about it." He heard her bang the cleaver, punctuating her words. "Carl is just a friend . . . a *friend*, Mercer. This is *my* house, and I can invite anyone I want."

He clicked off the bathroom light to go to his bedroom to finish dressing, but suddenly, she was blocking the doorway, her hands on her hips. "I am so sick of your bullshit, Mercer. I'm calling everyone to cancel. I'll say you've been called away on a family matter. I just can't go on with this farce any longer. You need to get out now!" She was shrieking, her face purple with rage.

Tibodeau lunged at his wife, reaching out to silence her spewing lips. Claire swung her arm in an arc, hitting him hard in the ear with the flat of her hand. He reacted by roughly covering her mouth, forcing her across the hall and into the wall. Mercer's hands slid from her face and tightened around her throat. In spite of his wife's clawing defense, unaffected by the terror in her eyes, he continued his vice-like grip. More quickly than he would ever have imagined, those eyes rolled back and the struggling ceased. As a reflex, Tibodeau held onto his wife so that the sudden weight of her inert body pulled him to the floor. He was panting, his ear throbbing from her blow, as he scrambled to his knees and felt the pulse-point at her neck. Nothing. He pounded on her chest a half dozen times and then checked again for a pulse. Claire's heart was still — Tibodeau's beat wildly. Sitting back hard against the wall, he looked beyond his wife's pale form and into the living room where mellow, mote-filled sunlight swirled down from a skylight. His mind raced forward through the day to the hour when the guests would arrive. He would have to spring into action as soon as his shaking legs would support him.

Raleigh was totally lost, but at least the soft light of early morning sun afforded her safe footing on the uneven surface.

Humidity glued her wheat-colored hair to her temples and the nape of her neck. Scanning the sides of the road, she noticed a long downhill drive covered with pine needles and caught a glimpse of an immense roofline through the trees. Raleigh walked toward the other end of the drive to where it intersected with a properly paved road.

A silver SUV idled on the shoulder there. "Thank God," Raleigh thought, "someone must be at home here." Then she noticed the silhouette of two men inside the vehicle and suddenly felt uneasy.

Before she could react, the sound of car doors groaning open sent a startled flock of birds clacking from beneath a magnolia's broad, shiny leaves. Then a blur of blue oxford shirt was on her and Raleigh went down on one knee in the weeds with a sharp cry. She tried to look up in protest, but a man forced her head to her chest, roughly pulling her arms behind her. A second figure lashed a pungent piece of tape across her mouth, catching and pulling her hair. She felt tape winding around her wrists. A dark cloth sack was placed over her head; a ragged hole had been cut at nose level.

Raleigh forced air through her nose with a loud rasping sound as the men dragged her back to the running vehicle. Through the bottom of the sack she could see the scuffed black shoes and khaki pants of one of the men as he pushed her into the back seat. She curled up on her side. A lightweight cloth or blanket was tossed over her. Still slightly drunk from the night before, Raleigh felt queasy. The rocking and swaying of the car as it sped away disoriented her. Neither man said a single word. The car's engine and the loud whirring of the cicadas high in the canopy canceled out Raleigh's muffled cries for help.

🍂 🍂 🍂

In the house at the end of the pine-needled drive, the Oriental rug in the dining room swam into Mercer Tibodeau's consciousness. He pushed himself up the wall, walked over to it on trembling legs, seizing on the idea that it was the perfect size to conceal his wife's body for transport. He pulled himself together and finished the preparations for the party, but only partially. He planned to claim later that his wife completed most of the cooking and setting up before she walked over to the church for the eight A.M. services, as was her custom. He gathered up her purse and the Sunday school outfit she had hanging in her dressing room, along with shoes and stockings, and threw them onto the carpet with the body. He scattered her make-up bottles and vials around the counter of her bathroom. The guests for the party would arrive to find the police taking a missing person report from the distraught husband.

Acres of his wife's estate had recently been sold off for a development of shoulder-to-shoulder McMansions, netting millions. There were still almost three acres of wooded lot between their massive Tudor and the nearest neighbor, but Tibodeau was careful to do everything with the three-car garage doors closed. After pulling on some overalls and collecting the required items from his workroom, he loaded the car's trunk with the rolled up carpet, its contents, and a small shovel. He placed his loafers on the car seat, but wore a pair of gardening clogs. He backed the Lexus out of the long, serpentine drive by rote, cautiously traversing the sleepy neighborhood, much of which stood on property previously owned by the family for almost two centuries. Bordering the Dismal Swamp, the land back then had been cypress timber-rich, and when that was all cut, hemp was the cash crop. For fifty years, until he was too old and feeble, Tibodeau's father had been the resident groundskeeper. Mercer held the job for years after that, until he won Claire's hand in marriage, much to the horror of her family.

Tibodeau eased his car into a shallow ravine behind a stand of lilac bushes laced with yellow honeysuckle. He opened the trunk, hoisted the tube of carpet over his shoulder, and followed an ancient path made by game coursing through the undergrowth, nearly imperceptible to anyone who had not grown up on the estate. His thoughts went back to summers during grade school when he brought empty canning jars with perforated lids into these woods. He'd capture fireflies at dusk for his own late-night light show in his room in the caretaker's cottage. Tibodeau snapped back to the present as he carefully crossed a creek foul with stagnant water, balancing himself on large stones, shifting the long bundle like the pole of a circus tightrope walker. As his head cleared the slight rise of the embankment, graceful dragonflies with jeweled wings hovered around him. Scanning the area, he wiped the sweat from his sparse eyebrows onto the sleeve of his shirt, then walked through a tall stand of pines to denser underbrush just beyond.

When he was certain that no one could see him, he dropped the rug, knelt on it to keep the clay loam from staining his pants, and dug a hole in the sodden earth. Thinking that the rug made the perfect makeshift coffin for his wife, he maneuvered it into the shallow grave, completely covering it with dirt and pine straw. He stood and surveyed the area to make sure nothing could be detected, walking backward to see how the site looked from a distance. Traveling a different route home down a little used road, he prepared what he would say to the authorities. Halfway across a one-lane bridge he lowered the car window, breathed in the rich, sultry air of the brackish water below, and judging it to be the perfect resting place for his soiled gardening clogs and shovel, tossed them out.

r r r

Raleigh lost all track of time as they bumped along. The car finally stopped, its hot metal parts clicking as she waited for what would come next. Rough, gloved hands helped her out of the back seat and marched her across a patch of weeds and skimpy grass, her strappy party sandals catching in the leaves and debris. She stumbled up metal latticework stairs, and once inside, the floor rocked. A trailer. Scuffed-black-shoes man steered her down a short hall into a stuffy room.

The man said, "Kneel here, Mrs. Tibodeau."

Raleigh's knees touched a thin, bare mattress. When the man slammed the door, she lay down. "Mrs. Tibodeau? Mrs. Tibodeau? Who do they think I am?" Hot tears of frustration ran down her face and across the smelly tape. If they would peel it off and let her speak, she would explain that they had the wrong person. Raleigh fought feelings of panic and imminent suffocation. She rocked back and forth, back and forth, in the steamy closeness of the sealed room.

Mercer Tibodeau's daydream was disturbed by the harping of the phone on his desk. He readied himself to pile on the drama if the church director was calling to ask why his wife hadn't shown up for services. He rehearsed his speech in his head a little too long — the recorder on his answering machine activated, "You have reached 757-481- . . . ." He jabbed at the *off* button and said, "Hello," momentarily fumbling the receiver.

"Mr. Tibodeau?" asked a distant-sounding voice.

"Yes . . . speak up please."

"We have your wife," was the nearly incomprehensible reply.

"You have her *what*?" Tibodeau sputtered. He squinted in an effort to understand, noticing then that the conversation was still being recorded by the answering machine.

"Listen carefully." The man's heavily muffled words continued without inflection. "Don't contact the police or newspapers. We won't hurt her if you do as we tell you. We suggest you handle this . . . this situation solo, pal!"

Instructions about the dollar amount and the delivery of the ransom followed, which Tibodeau wrote down in the margins of a flyer he found on the kitchen counter. It advertised the best deep dish pizza in the low country. He was playing along, buying time to work out what was really happening. Had the caller seen him bury his wife? Was this a blackmailer on the line?

"What the hell is this? What have you done with my wife? Let me talk to her." This last question could have been a gamble, since the kidnappers couldn't put his wife on the phone, but Tibodeau wanted his recorded expressions of concern to sound authentic on the tape.

He paced up and down the wide plank floor of the kitchen. "Not one damned cent until I hear her say that she's all right," he said through clenched teeth, really getting into his role. A vacuum of silence sucked all the life out of the phone line.

Eventually the kidnapper continued. "We'll put her on. As

long as you do your part, man, and keep this between us, we can be accomodatin', we can be nice. We have an understanding, am I right?"

𝗿 𝗿 𝗿

When the door to the stifling little room was thrown open, Raleigh drew back against the wall. She was pulled to a standing position, her hood lifted up to her nose, the saliva-soaked tape peeled from her mouth.

"I brought water," the man said as he held the cup for her. Raleigh could not feel her mouth, couldn't form words to explain things to him, or place her lips correctly on the rim of the cup, so that much of its water streamed down her front. That which she could swallow was such an unexpected joy, tears filled her eyes beneath the hood.

𝗿 𝗿 𝗿

Was it a prank or would they really put a woman on the phone and expect me not to know my own wife? he wondered. The caller sounded sincere. *What a colossal screw up this kidnapper is, then. And some ransom demand. Two hundred thousand dollars for the return of my wife? Out of an estate worth at least 3.5 million dollars?* Of which he was now the sole beneficiary. Could there be such a cosmic joke as a kidnapper dialing the wrong number? Then it occurred to him. The kidnapper must have cased their property and watched his wife leaving for church early on Sunday mornings. The unlucky bitch they grabbed must resemble his wife. What the hell had the woman been doing near their house that early in the morning? Where was her car? No matter. He was obviously dealing with a real amateur — the kidnapper didn't even realize he was being recorded.

When the woman finally came to the phone, Tibodeau was startled. In his calculating state of mind, he had forgotten that he still held the handset to his ear.

A shaky voice whispered, "Please . . . please just do as they say."

Tibodeau wondered how this woman was going to react

when she realized she was not speaking to her husband. "Are you . . . all right?" he asked the stranger.

There was a slight hesitation and Tibodeau thought he heard a sigh of relief from the woman. "I will be if you follow the instructions . . . please." So she was playing along as well.

The kidnapper came back on the line and warned Tibodeau again not to contact anyone and then . . . dial tone.

Tibodeau rooted around the utility room until he found an empty canvas bag and headed for the office safe, delaying his plan to call the police to report the kidnapping.

At the thought of replaying the message tape later for the cops, Tibodeau's thin lips stretched into a smile. This woman on the phone, this wife, was a complication on the one hand. On the other, a gift.

r r r

Raleigh stood inside her little prison. "We're leaving now," the man explained. He pressed his knuckles into the small of her back and guided her down the hall to the doorway where they all descended the swaying steps, one man on either side of her.

A few minutes later she was back on the floorboard of the sweltering car. An insistent voice, which she usually ignored when it concerned her husband, Guy, until too late, was warning her not to say anything now. Not to tell the kidnappers that she wasn't who they thought she was — no telling how they might react if they found out. The voice urged her to hold onto the hope that the man on the phone had his reasons for playing along and would continue to do so.

"I never saw their faces," she also thought, "and that will save me."

Finally the car stopped. Raleigh was pulled out and dragged through pine straw and leaves full of jumping insects, then seated between two huge, twisted roots of an ancient oak tree. The sound of the slow idle of a car off to her left and men talking in low, serious tones heightened her apprehension. Abruptly, scuffed black shoes fled past her, followed by the second man. Doors slammed and the car sped away.

Slow and deliberate steps came toward her. Raleigh prepared to fight for all she was worth. Her hands were cut free of the tape, the hood removed.

The sudden wash of sunlight seared to the core of her skull, her arms were so heavy and useless that she could not cover her eyes. She knew she should get away from this man, this *husband*, until she figured out what part he played in her abduction, but as he lifted her from the ground she could only hang limply in his arms, accepting that her dreams of saving herself were a fantasy.

He placed her gently on the back seat of his car with its sweet chilled air and its new-car smell. She tried to catch his eyes in the rearview mirror to gauge his intent, but he only looked at the road.

"It will all be over soon," he said.

At the sound of his calm voice, Raleigh continued to hope. She allowed her head to sink back against the seat. She watched the cloudless summer sky through the rear window as the car sailed down the road.

Tibodeau retraced his journey across the one-lane bridge, heading once more toward the deep woods, the pine stand, and the freshly turned soil in the underbrush.

Logan, as she prefers to be called, has lived in Virginia since 1985, spending her formative years in the Deep South — a setting that still informs her writing and its themes. This rich cross-pollination, the sultry clime of southern marshlands with the bountiful Chesapeake and its culture, enriches her art.

Logan toils full time to be the best writer possible, finding challenge and a home in the crime fiction community. The first book of her traditional mystery series, *The Sighing Pine Murders*, is in the final-edit stage.

THE LOCKBOX

by G.M. Malliet

It was one of the nicest homes Walter De Sales had seen in all his years of selling real estate. One of a row of Federalist-style, four-story townhouses built in the eighties to replace the government's World War II riverside warehouses, it was small — less than 3,000 square feet — but crafted to an illusion of sunlit spaciousness. It had withstood occupancy by a number of owners, the D.C. area being a place few called home for long. Priced in 1987 at $275,000, it now listed for $1,100,000, due in part to its picture-postcard views of the Potomac and the Maryland shoreline from the upper floors.

It was amazing, really. His mother had told him that fifty years ago, this entire block had been a vacant lot where the cops found bums frozen to death every winter.

Walter double-checked the computer printout for 103 Enderley Street. The house would open for public viewing the next day.

"Shows well. This one won't last!" For once, the listing agent's description was a model of understatement. If it weren't for the faint scuff mark on the wallpaper by the top of the stairs, Walter would have agreed.

He got back to work with the soap and water.

r r r

Some hours earlier, Walter had let himself into the marble foyer of the house. He used a programmed access card — about the size of a credit card — that released the house key from the gray lockbox hanging on the front doorknob. A computer somewhere in Minnesota recorded the time as 17:04:07 P.M. EST. Each night, he and his colleagues had to reset their cards by docking them in a special device connected to this central computer. That way a lost or stolen card was quickly rendered useless to thieves.

The funny thing was, Walter thought, it was harder in the old, low-tech days — when only the listing agent held the physical key to the house — to have the freedom of access he now enjoyed. The computer never recorded when he left a property; he could theoretically stay all day and night, for weeks on end, if he wanted, with no one the wiser.

Locking the door behind him, Walter noticed that the enameled Chinese table in the foyer already held two dozen business cards from his colleagues and competitors, added just since the noon opening. Carefully, he added his own card to the pile. The ritual was a courtesy to other agents, so everyone could gauge the interest in a property.

Walter had talked for a few minutes with the listing agent at the lunchtime brokers' open. As usual, Sam Burley had lured other agents with the promise of food, wine, and a drawing for a gift certificate, to jumpstart the sale. Completely unnecessary, in Walter's opinion. The house would sell itself, even in the current anemic market.

Brandishing a chardonnay, Sam had told Walter the owners — a Mr. and Mrs. Kyle Hoffman — were at their new home in Middleburg for the Labor Day weekend, wishing to avoid the parade trooping through their home. Most owners chose to escape viewings, a fact Walter had found useful over the years. He was always careful to leave no trace, after all. What was the harm in pretending that such a beautiful house might have been — should have been — his?

He had always loved houses — other people's houses, other people's lives. Lives with, as he imagined, wonderful secrets. He could, in a house like this one, pretend he was wealthy, that he had excellent taste and style, pretend — most of all — that he was living someone else's life, with lots of attractive, successful friends over for gourmet meals and witty conversation two or three times a month. In this life there would be a purebred dog by the fireplace, a thoroughbred blonde at Walter's side, literature and art ranged along the walls. There were often children in this scenario, a boy and a girl, playing checkers in complete silence in a distant room. That Walter liked neither dogs, women, nor children was beside the point. Although conventionally handsome in an insipid, sandy-haired way that reminded people of Dan Quayle, neither dogs nor women, on extended acquaintance, seemed to like him either. Children shied from him like colts.

But in his new life, these props were necessary accouterments. Somewhat like the sculpture these people, the Hoffmans, owned. He stopped at the foot of a short flight of steps leading into the house proper. To his left, a carved stone bust rested atop a marble pedestal. He stopped to caress the top of its head. He wasn't sure who it was supposed to be. Some bearded Roman. Maybe Plato or Socrates. Or were they Greek? Anyway, in his new life, touches of culture like Socrates would be essential.

＊ ＊ ＊

Walter's fantasy life had started in earnest when his mother died, nearly ten years before. For a long time he mourned her, staying up late, watching infomercials on TV. One night he bought a donut maker that still sat in his garage, collecting dust. It was out of pure boredom and loneliness, really, that he went into real estate.

He started calling agents about houses he saw advertised in the paper. He'd give a phony name, make up a job and phone number if necessary, and arrange a private showing. He'd had to be careful not to arrange viewings too often, and never in his own neighborhood. And, of course, never with the same agent for too long.

He quickly realized open houses were better — if there were several house-hunters there to keep the agent occupied, Walter was often left alone long enough to rummage through drawers, open closets, and generally learn everyone's secrets. Bookshelves and video cases were very revealing. Medicine cabinets, too. The family photos were a gold mine: someone's no-hope punk graduating from junior high, or Uncle Horace drunkenly carving a Thanksgiving turkey. He warned his clients to hide everything before they put their houses on the market, but so many didn't listen. They simply didn't understand that buying a house was all about fantasy, about people climbing the social ladder, about people projecting themselves onto the screen of a better, happier, luckier life.

After a few months of skulking about at open houses, Walter realized the only way to feed his lust — there was no other word for it — for peering into other people's closets was to become an agent himself, like his mother. He once had ignored all her nagging on the subject, but now he acknowledged how perfectly suited he was for the job. He'd barely had to study to pass the exam, having learned the ins and outs of contracts, deposits, inspections, and deeds at her knee. He made a fair living at it, even during the inevitable market downswings. He'd even come up with a catchy slogan for his advertising: *Walter de Sales Sells!* boasted the newspaper ads beside his photo, in which he smiled his anxious-to-please, somewhat desperate agent's smile. But money wasn't the point. Even though — and Walter never understood why — his mother had cut him out of her will in favor of Habitat for Humanity, money wasn't Walter's problem.

He gave Socrates a final pat and walked up the steps into one of the formal living areas. On the printout, it was called The Library. The space opened to reveal bookcases built into two walls and a fireplace against the far wall, also framed by bookcases. With the shelves and cabinets, as with everything else, the owner had spared no expense — these were real hardwood built-ins, not fiberfill junk hammered together by some weekend carpenter. The attention to detail showed even in the doorknobs — the owner had replaced the builder's standard metal ones throughout with antique glass or brass knobs.

Brocade draperies the color of brandy covered the fourth wall. Earlier, during the broker's open, Sam had pulled these drapes open with a showman's flourish, and the sight of the brick patio beyond had nearly brought a tear to Walter's eye. The area was small, exquisitely landscaped, bordered with jewel-like clusters of late summer plants that gleamed more softly now in the later afternoon light. A high brick wall provided privacy, and two manicured evergreens in large terracotta pots further shielded the view of neighbors to either side. In the fall, a Japanese maple would provide a red canopy of near-total seclusion.

While the patio was too intimate for a large gathering, still it spoke to Walter of what he thought of as Gracious Living. He could see himself lounging on the teak chairs after a long day at work, the nagging voice that ruled his existence blessedly stilled, a drink in one hand and a cigarette in the other, Nick Charles awaiting his Nora.

The only thing marring the scene was a rectangular fish pond that was filled to six inches from the rim with dirt. Walter stood beside it, puzzled — he'd meant to ask Sam about it during the open but couldn't get near him again for the crowd. Now he saw, partially hidden behind a flowering plant in a large clay tub, three bags of cement and a pallet of bricks.

"Nice, isn't it?"

Walter nearly jumped out of his loafers. Sam Burley seemed to have materialized out of nowhere. The man moved like a cat. A 200-pound cat with an expensive toupee and capped teeth.

Walter was sure he'd locked the front door. Sam must have a separate set of keys to the place.

"Didn't mean to surprise you," Sam said smoothly. "Someone left the back gate to the alley open. I noticed it as I was driving by." He surveyed the pleasant scene with a proprietary air. "They have a gardener come in twice a month. Imagine, for this small a garden. So," he turned to Walter, "you couldn't stay away, huh? Got a buyer in mind?"

"What's the concrete for?" Walter asked, annoyed at the scare, and the interruption.

Sam took out one of his foul-smelling cigars and began the elaborate ritual of clipping and lighting it. In between puffs, using the cigar for punctuation, he said:

"The owner wanted to replace the pond with an outdoor fireplace. He started the work himself, then decided to sell. Divorce in the works, if you ask me." Puff. "It's gotta be divorce when they start doing expensive home improvements. That, or trying for a baby." Puff. "Anyway, these ponds are the devil to keep clean. The leaves fall in, the pump clogs up . . . it's endless. I convinced him it could add $15K to the asking price with an outdoor fireplace so he decided to go ahead with it."

"What's he do?" Walter asked.

"For a living? Lawyer. Both him and the wife. Money for nothin'. Hah!"

That figured, Walter thought. They had to be rolling in it if they had already closed on one house with another barely on the market.

"It'll ruin the showing," Walter said.

"Nah. I've got two guys coming by late tonight to pour concrete over the dirt and gravel. Tomorrow they'll get started on the brickwork. It might not be completely finished by next week but enough that people can get the general idea." He looked at his watch. "Gotta dash. Don't forget to lock up."

"How late?" Walter asked. "I mean, when will the workers get here?"

A more perceptive man might have noticed the anxiety in Walter's voice. Sam was only perceptive where potential buyers were concerned.

"Nine, maybe later. First they have to finish up another job for me."

Walter relaxed. He would have a couple of hours to himself, anyway.

r r r

"A man's home is his castle," Walter liked to tell his clients. It was a concept his mother had never understood, of course. But then, as she frequently had pointed out, it was her house he was living in, not his.

He couldn't remember now when he'd taken the very short journey from pretending houses and lives were his to wanting other people to believe they were. Two years ago? Three?

It was easy to find stray women in D.C. bars, anonymous places where he could adopt a name and a new persona for a few hours. The kind of place where nobody knew your name. He was well-dressed, nice-looking. He drove a late-model SUV he kept spit-polished. Selling real estate had given him a line in smooth, pointless banter.

He'd convince the women to meet him at the house. Sometimes the same night; more often the next day. He needed time to get the lockbox off and survey the premises. Since houses on the market were usually "staged," on the advice of the agent — the industry term for removing any trace of messy, real, human habitation — it was surprisingly simple. People believed what they wanted to believe, in Walter's experience. Why, after all, would anyone lie about owning a house?

It was easy. So easy it worried him. But even though there was much to remember, and much that could go wrong, Walter was good at double- and triple-checking everything. He'd hide photos and agents' cards and anything else that could give the game away. Of course, it only worked when the home owner was a single male. Still, he was amazed how gullible women could be. How their eyes lit up at the first sight of his beautiful home!

Well, there had been that one. The memory of *that* close call still sent a frisson of alarm along his spine. She'd been suspicious when he couldn't find the brandy, and when he fumbled with the light switch. He'd finally had to "confess" it was his cousin's house. The explanation seemed to satisfy her — just. But it had been a near thing. He was more careful after that.

The Hoffmans' was too obviously a couple's house. It wouldn't do. Still, the thought of several hours on his own to sit by the bedroom fireplace was happiness enough. He'd try on Hoffman's colognes, maybe pour himself a glass of wine, if a bottle were open in the fridge, or a small brandy. He'd planned to take a bath in the Jacuzzi, but thanks to Sam and his workmen, he wasn't sure he should chance it.

Of course, he'd be careful to clean up after himself. They'd never know. They never did.

◤ ◤ ◤

"You might have told me she was coming here." Brenda Hoffman put down the pile of clothes she'd taken from her suitcase, the better to glare at her husband. They had been married seven years, the point at which differences between couples either disappear or become unbearable.

"I told you," her husband said, over the top of his newspaper. "The drains in her house are backed up. She can't use the sinks or even take a decent shower. She only asked if she could stay with us a few days, when she can get someone out to look at it."

Brenda, though a small woman, was imposing. Many a

prosecutor had quailed when she drew herself up to her full five feet, one inch, as she did now.

"No plumber takes three days to come out and look at a clogged drain, for Pete's sake. The only clog is in her arteries. Can't she stay in a hotel?"

Kyle Hoffman inhaled and then sighed deeply, puffing out his cheeks. It made him look like one of those allegorical wind heads drawn on antique maps. It was a huge sigh that spoke of a man, world weary, who had carried far too large a burden for far too long. It was the sigh that Brenda decided, in retrospect, made her snap. As if what she were asking were some *big* deal.

"She's my mother," he said. "What the hell do you want me to do?"

"I want — I thought this weekend was — this house . . ."

Oh, what was the use? After seven years, their arguments on the subject had become so predictable they might as well have recorded them and replayed the tape several times a month. Next, he would say, "Look. We're all the family she's got." And Brenda would say, "Doesn't she have a friend *somewhere* she could stay with?" And he would say, "What few friends she had are long gone." "Sure. Driven to an early grave by her nit-picking." "That's really cruel, you know. She's 70 years old, for chrissake." "She'll live to bury both of us." "Brenda . . . " (This last said in a warning tone.) "No. I've had it, Kyle."

What she wanted was for Kyle to put his foot down when his mother played the widow/guilt card. What she wanted was . . . a marriage. Not this three-legged arrangement where she, Brenda, spent half her free time waiting on the old bat hand and foot. To make matters worse, the old lady was going deaf, so you had to repeat everything at least twice. As a twisted bonus, she also seemed to have suffered some memory loss in recent years, so she often told you the same story, loudly, four times. Being with her for a weekend was like being stuck in a madhouse with an echo chamber.

"What I want," Brenda finally said, resolved to switch tactics, "is for you two to have a lovely weekend. I'm going back to Alexandria. I'm going *home*. See you next week. Or not. Frankly, Kyle, I don't give a damn."

"Brenda —"

She picked up her purse and began noisily rummaging through it, looking for her keys. Kyle, watching her — her face red, her lips thin with anger, her expensively highlighted hair disheveled — had a sudden revelation: He no longer cared. Seven years of this crap. It was as if Brenda, all along, had been forcing him to choose. Silently, he chose.

She was still talking, not noticing her audience was checking his watch.

"You promised me this would be a new start. That's what you said. We moved out here to get away from her, didn't we?" She waited for an answer, but he sat mutely, not meeting her eyes. She had the thought — ridiculous thought — that he was just waiting for her to leave so he could return to his newspaper.

This was new; it unnerved her. Kyle always loved a good argument.

Somehow it all reminded her of the times in court when she was sure a witness was lying, but she wasn't sure why.

Still, she plowed on. "It's a different house, but the same deal. So let her stay here as long as she wants. Just don't expect *me* to stay, too."

🔫 🔫 🔫

It is a little over an hour's drive from Middleburg to Alexandria. Brenda, traveling much too fast, came off Spout Run with ten minutes to spare. As she connected with GW Parkway, she caught a glimpse of the dark spires of Georgetown to the left, looming majestically over the Potomac. Normally it was a sight to fill her with peace and wonder, but she drove in a kind of blind panic, the memory of Kyle's impassive face before her eyes. Somewhere midway, around Oakton, she'd finally accepted that, with an inevitability that had been there from the first day, the marriage was over. She'd written Kyle a note to that effect before she'd left, telling him she was leaving for good, that her attorney would be in touch. This she had signed and dated with a lawyerly flourish. It had seemed like an opening bid at the time. Now she knew it was the whole deal.

Okay. So maybe she'd move to New York. Or maybe she'd

go back to the small town in Maine where she started from. Start a practice there.

The great thing about being a lawyer was, crime is everywhere.

Twenty minutes later, she pulled up in front of the townhouse. Someone had left a light on in the master bedroom.

God damn stupid real estate agents.

🮢 🮢 🮢

Walter was in the master bedroom watching a video of *Dude, Where's My Car?* when he heard the key turn in the front door lock. Quickly, he hit the Stop button. He turned off the light on the nightstand, plunging the house into darkness.

Damn. Sam was here with the workmen already?

🮢 🮢 🮢

The lower house was dark, but Brenda knew the house like the back of her hand. It wasn't until she reached the bottom of the stairs that she turned on the lights. At the same moment, Walter turned off the bedroom light.

What the heck, she thought. Had that agent — what was his name, Sam? — been messing with the electricity for some reason?

At the first landing, looking up, she saw the outline of a dark figure looming in the bedroom door.

She screamed, took a step backward. Her heel caught the edge of the step and snapped with the sound of a small bone breaking; her other shoe scuffed the wall as she fought for balance.

She tumbled back down the stairs.

🮢 🮢 🮢

There was no question she was dead. Those staring eyes. . . .

He stood staring back, disbelieving. Her neck . . . that couldn't be right.

No, no, that couldn't be right.

His mind gibbered with the question of what to do. He couldn't just carry her out of the house; it was too risky, even in darkness. He couldn't leave her where she was, that was certain. Losing his license would be the least of it. There was no way to explain. . . .

He'd already been in the house for three hours. But only the computer knew that. So long as no human being knew, he was fine. No one could know how long he'd stayed.

But . . . the lockbox did know he was the last person to enter the house. They'd find the body, and. . . .

What had Sam said, they'd be here at nine or so?

He couldn't let them find her. Or him.

That's when he remembered the pond.

🔫 🔫 🔫

In forty minutes, it was done, the earth tamped back over the small body, which lay nearly folded in half beneath. Her hair, bleached into multi-colored stripes of blonde and brown, had fanned against the floor of her grave like the pelt of a wild animal. It was that he would remember, when he thought of her hiding place.

He scattered the displaced dirt around the base of the shrubbery, likewise tamping it down to conceal the new disturbance. Tools from the garage — shovel, rake, broom, garden hose — helped him finish the night's work. He wiped his prints off the garden equipment, thinking his prints elsewhere in the house could easily be explained. It was then he remembered the video. Racing back upstairs, he removed it from the machine and stored it back in its jacket, again being careful to wipe off his prints.

He stole a peek from behind the bedroom curtains. The neighboring houses remained dark. He was alone, unobserved. He'd burn the clothes he was wearing, just to be safe.

He'd gotten away with it.

🔫 🔫 🔫

"Honey, come look at this patio!"

Herb Granger dutifully followed his wife's voice to the rear of the house at 103 Enderly Street. It was like walking out of a dark movie theater into the sunshine, and it took a few minutes for his eyes to adjust.

"There's just the right light for geraniums over there," she told him. Gladys fancied herself quite the gardener. "I wonder why the planters are on this concrete platform thing — it looks silly."

"It's only temporary," said Sam Burley, who'd followed them out. "It was meant to be the foundation for an outdoor fireplace, but the husband never had the brickwork done once the concrete was poured over the dirt. There was . . . some upset in the family awhile back and he just lost interest. Wife disappeared, or something."

At the looks on their faces, he added hastily, "Oh, nothing to do with this house. No, nothing like that. She just left him. Told him she was running off. Who knows, maybe she met someone. Happens all the time."

Herb, who didn't believe a woman could be so considerate, merely grunted.

"The police weren't suspicious?"

"Nah. Her folks had them look into it, but the husband had a solid alibi and a good lawyer, and no one else had a motive. Besides, the wife left a Dear John letter or something. They reckon she'll turn up when she's ready. Like I said, I see it all the time in this business."

In fact, Sam had gathered from news accounts that the police had raked the husband over the coals, only leaving him alone once he'd passed two lie detector tests. But there was no need to go into the sordid details with these nice people from Ohio. He could tell from the gleam in her eyes the wife was ready to make a written offer. It only remained to persuade her husband. The sorry marital squabbles of the previous owners couldn't be allowed to come into it.

Since the guy looked like he might have some more questions, Sam rushed on:

"Anyway, you can put a barbeque there, or one of those portable gas fireplaces. It's better this way, really. Gives you lots of options."

"How sad," Gladys said, not really listening. She'd already made up her mind to have this house and a little scandal about the previous owners wasn't going to stop her. She stood, measuring the concrete slab with her eyes.

"You know, if we dug it all up, it could make a nice fish pond, don't you think?"

G.M. Malliet has worked as a journalist and copywriter for national and international news publications and broadcasters. Her education included graduate study in England at the University of Cambridge and Oxford University.

Her first mystery, *Death of a Cozy Writer*, set in Cambridgeshire, won the Malice Domestic grant. It will be published in July 2008 by Midnight Ink. The second novel in the St. Just series, *Death and the Lit Chick*, will be published in 2009.

Her first short story, "The Bartender," appeared in the *Chesapeake Crimes 2* anthology.

She and her husband live in Virginia.

CROSSING THE BRIDGE

by Carolyn Mulford

"Sorry nothing exciting happened, Mrs. Morris," Corporal Picatti said as he parked at the edge of the diner's empty, unlit lot. "Queen Anne's County really does have crime."

"I'm delighted not to have seen any." Lucille's heart rate decelerated toward normal as she gave thanks for surviving the ride-along without disgracing herself and, more important, her rookie cop daughter.

The pink neon EATS on the roof blinked on and off as they hurried through a salt-tinged mist toward the small frame building. Lucille regretted that the deputy had bypassed three fine seafood restaurants earlier, their windows doubtless framing the sun setting over the Chesapeake. This place faced two shuttered shops across a dark street.

The tall, dark, and talkative deputy held the glass door open for her. "They fix baked rockfish better than my mother, and their crabmeat cakes go light on the bread and heavy on the Tabasco. None of those bound-for-the-beach crab burgers here."

Lucille's appetite rose at the smell of crab cakes — and receded at the sight of black duct-tape patches on six stools lined up along a dingy, gray counter. A round, plastic case holding slices of cake and pie stood at the end of the counter. No one sat in the booths behind the stools or the ones to Lucille's left.

A teenager with spiked orange hair and an old-fashioned blue apron rose from the last stool and came toward them in the duck walk of impending motherhood. "The cook already left. I can't give you nothing but crab cakes or hamburgers."

Lucille didn't care. She just wanted a safe place to wait until Jackie could pick her up. "How late are you open?"

"Until 10 o'clock."

Another hour. Plenty of time. Lucille turned left toward the cleanest looking of four low-backed booths. Their faux leather seats also bore duct tape.

"Back in a minute," the deputy said, pushing open a door with a fake buoy on it. The men's room.

Lucille headed toward the door bearing a carving of a gull. Her spirits edged up as she smelled disinfectant and saw the spotless tile floor. A clean bathroom meant a clean kitchen. She tended to her first priority and retrieved her cell phone to call Jackie.

"How did the ride-along go, Mom? Did you catch any killers?"

"Most of it was rather boring, actually." Or would have been if she hadn't been terrified every minute. She'd endured it in hopes of understanding why Jackie had quit a secure state job to join the Annapolis police force. "We went to a house where the burglar alarm went off accidentally. Mostly we checked traffic." She must say something positive. "I got to hold the radar gun, but it was rush hour when nobody could speed. We just came from watching for shoplifters on twenty little TVs in a back room at a Queenstown outlet. That was fun." Almost.

"Sounds like a pretty typical shift. Where shall I pick you up?"

"A diner just south of Centreville. It has a pink neon EATS sign."

"I know the place. Get a piece of apple pie to go for me, please. They make it with pineapple juice, an old recipe. If they're out, I'll settle for the black walnut cake."

The diner obviously had better food than ambiance. "When will you be here?"

"Between 9:45 and 9:50."

"Then I won't worry about you until 9:52," Lucille joked. Jackie never came late, and she never wasted time.

"If you'd stop closing your eyes and curling into a fetal position every time you cross the Bay Bridge, you could have driven yourself, and I wouldn't be losing sleep coming to get you."

Lucille shuddered at the thought of the long, high arch and the deep water below. Not wanting her two daughters to grow up as timid as she was, she'd succeeded in hiding most of her fears, but not that one. Both girls had become disconcertingly fearless adults.

"I'll be watching so you won't lose time by coming in for me. Love you, sweetie." She put the phone back in her purse.

A mosquito buzzed around her head. She clapped her hands at it and, to her dismay, opened them to a squished mess. She washed her hands and punched the button on the world's loudest dryer. Above it she heard a door close, a man shout, and two pops. She froze.

A woman screamed.

The dryer clicked off.

Footsteps sounded nearby. "You in the restroom! Come out with your hands up! Right now!"

Lucille couldn't move, couldn't breathe, couldn't speak.

"Right now," the man snarled, "or — or I'll start shooting."

Lucille forced herself to breathe. Play it like when Jackie brought home that snake. Don't show how scared you are. But could he hear her heart thumping? She stepped through the door with her damp hands up and her purse dangling from her right shoulder.

Two big pistols pointed at her. The man behind them wore black except for a white diamond on the ski mask covering his head. He backed toward the front door, bouncing on his toes like a boxer and waving the guns between the teenager behind the counter and Lucille.

"Okay, Carrot Top. Take the money out of the cash register and put it on the counter."

The teenager gasped a sob, hit some keys, and opened the register. She put several bills on the counter.

The gunman stuck one gun — the deputy's service revolver — into the right-hand pocket of his hooded sweatshirt and spread the money out while pointing the other gun at Lucille. "Jesus! That's all ones and fives. Where's the rest at?"

"That's all of it. I swear! We never keep more than $50 after 8 o'clock." Wiping tears away, the girl looked at the floor in front of Lucille. "Is he . . . is he dead?"

For a moment, Lucille — mesmerized by the gun — didn't understand the question. She lowered her gaze. Corporal Picatti lay on his back, blood streaming from a gash over his right eye. A hole the size of a button marred his light-blue shirt, but no blood stained it. His vest had stopped a bullet. His chest rose.

The gunman bounced a step toward them. "Well, lady, is he dead or not?"

Lucille bent over as though to get a better look and debated whether to lie. If he thought he'd killed a cop, surely he'd run and she could call an ambulance. She went as far as she dared: "He looks dead."

"Holy crap! I didn't mean to kill him. He surprised me." The gunman grabbed the money and stuffed it in his pants pocket. "How much you got in that purse?"

"About $40. You're welcome to it."

He shook his head. "Damn it! Damn it all to hell!" He glanced out at the empty parking lot. "Okay. Toss your purse over here, and no funny business."

Her muscles weak as spent rubber bands, Lucille barely managed to heave the purse beyond the deputy's feet.

The gunman motioned for the teenager to join Lucille. "You both get against that back wall, and keep your hands up."

Starkly white under her orange hair, the teenager tiptoed past the deputy and fell against Lucille.

She caught the girl. "She's pregnant. She needs to sit down."

The gunman opened Lucille's purse. "Okay, okay. She can sit in that back booth." He found the cell phone and the wallet, took the cash, and pitched the purse behind the counter. Pocketing Lucille's cell phone, he crept up to the deputy, ripped off the radio unit on his shoulder, and pulled back. "You! Get the wallet out of his pocket."

A wave of heat moved up the back of Lucille's neck as she knelt by the deputy. She fought to stop it before it turned to dizziness. Taking slow, deep breaths, she ran her hand under Corporal Picatti's left hip. No wallet. His shirt pocket bulged. She unbuttoned it and drew out a wallet.

"How much he got?"

"Three twenties. Sixty dollars."

"Christ! I gotta have another hundred and fifty." He grabbed the money from her hand. "Hey! He's breathing." He pointed the gun at the deputy's head. "Don't move a

muscle. I don't wanna shoot you again, but I will if I have to."
He glared at Lucille. "You tried to trick me! Don't try it again.
I don't mind shooting a sneaky old woman."

Head swimming, she leaned against the wall. "He looked
dead. All that blood."

The deputy moaned.

The gunman bounced back three feet. "I know you're
faking. Get up!"

The wounded man opened his left eye and wiped away the
blood trickling into his right eye.

"Get up, or I'll shoot you *and* the old lady."

"Sure. Take it easy. I need a moment. I'm pretty woozy."
The deputy grasped the edge of the booth with his right hand
and pulled himself into a sitting position. Then he slumped
back to the floor.

The gunman watched without moving for several seconds.
He glanced outside. "Somebody could come any minute. Can't
leave him here." He shuffled his feet. "Okay. Carrot Top, get the
duct tape you use on these crummy seats."

She stumbled toward him, tears glistening on her cheeks.

As the young woman edged around the deputy, Lucille
read her name tag: Ronda. "It will be okay, Ronda," she said,
afraid for the girl and her baby. She looked around six months
along. "He just needs money. He doesn't want to hurt us." But
he certainly would.

"That's right," the gunman said. "I gotta have three hundred dollars by midnight. Do what I say and you'll be okay." He
bobbed backward to keep all of them in view.

Ronda went behind the counter, reached down, and
brought up a roll of duct tape.

"Tape his wrists together," he ordered, tugging at the
mouth of his ski mask.

Ronda knelt awkwardly. She wrapped the tape around the
deputy's wrists half a dozen times and tried to tear the end off
the roll.

"Leave it," the gunman said. "Now you two drag him into
the kitchen."

Lucille helped Ronda up and each grabbed an ankle. Hope
rose as they dragged Corporal Picatti over the black and red

tiles and into the kitchen. Maybe he'd come to and go out the back door for help. Maybe he had a shotgun in the trunk.

The gunman watched them from the kitchen door. "Okay, Carrot Top. Tape his wrists to the leg of that table. And do it good."

It was a metal worktable — bolted to the floor.

When Ronda finished, he motioned the women back into the dining room. "Carrot Top, you go sit in that back booth and keep your mouth shut. Old lady, you stand behind the counter by the cash register. And keep your hands where I can see them."

Lucille breathed deeply to steady herself as she moved to her assigned spot. She stared at the flashes of pink light outside. Her watch said 9:10. How long would the gunman wait for someone with $150? Few people carried much cash anymore. Surely a thief would know that. Maybe he was high on drugs. Maybe he was just plain stupid. Either one added to the danger.

He took a seat to her left on the last stool. His shoulders jiggled, and his hands made big lumps in his sweatshirt pockets. Gripping the guns, no doubt. She should think how to describe him to the police. A black blob with white sneakers. Slender. No, skinny. How tall? He'd seemed big at first when he was pointing those guns, but he probably was only about five feet nine. Big hands but hairless. A boy's hands.

"Get me a Coke," he said.

Lucille opened a small fridge under the counter. Canned Pepsi and bottled beer. She took out a can. "You want it in a glass with ice?"

"Just slide the damn can down here." He took his right hand out of his pocket to reach for it. "When somebody comes in, you tell them to sit in the booth right behind me. Got it?"

Lucille nodded. She leaned forward to see how Ronda was doing. She was sitting with her head on her arms.

Lights swung into the parking lot, showing the mist had turned into rain. The car parked in the space right outside the door.

The gunman pulled up his hood and hunched over the counter, but his right hand, the one away from the door, pointed a gun at Lucille.

She held her breath.

A tiny, white-haired, black woman got out on the passenger side and opened the door to the diner. Her smile created new wrinkles. "You got any applesauce cake left?"

Throat too tight to speak, Lucille nodded.

The woman turned and beckoned the driver.

Lucille cursed herself for not having the nerve to warn them away, but she choked out, "Have a seat in that last booth, please."

The driver, a foot taller than the woman, came in leaning heavily on a wood cane. He shuffled to the booth and eased himself down.

The gunman spun around. "Give me your cash, and you won't get hurt."

The two stared at him, mouths open, for a long moment. Then the woman reached into her large, black purse and took out a coin purse.

The gunman stood up. "You, too, mister."

The man reached into his pants pocket with an arthritic hand and brought out a silver money clip.

The gunman tossed the purse and clip on the counter. "Count it, old lady."

Lucille counted. "$29." Surely he'd give up and go.

He stuffed the money in his pants pocket and bounced back and forth between the door and the stool several times. "Okay. Make things look normal. Give them their cake."

Guilt mingling with fear, Lucille selected two pieces and carried them to the couple. "Don't worry," she said, both for them and the gunman. "He needs money. He doesn't want to hurt anyone."

The woman studied Lucille's face. "We understand." She pointed to the cake. "Could you bring us forks, please?"

"And we'd like coffee, ma'am," the man added. "Decaffeinated, please. Black."

"Certainly." Shamed by their calm, Lucille went behind the counter and poured steaming coffee into two sturdy, white mugs. She loaded those, forks, and napkins onto a dented, round metal tray and controlled her trembling well enough to deliver the coffee without spilling it. To ease tension, she said, "On the house."

The gunman snorted. "Real funny. Get back behind the counter." He looked toward the other end of the diner. "Hey, Carrot Top. Where's all your customers?"

Ronda raised her head. "We don't get many this late, especially when it rains."

Lucille put her hands on the counter. Surely he'd have sense enough to go.

"Old lady, give me a glass of ice."

She found a glass on a shelf and filled it from the ice dispenser. He must be burning up in that mask and sweatshirt, but obviously he felt in control, unafraid of a pregnant woman and three "old" people. He wasn't going to leave without $300. She slid the glass down the counter toward him and glanced at her watch. 9:25.

What if he still sat here when Jackie arrived? She feared nothing. She'd come in to see why Mom hadn't come out, and she'd take him on. He'd shoot her in an instant.

Panic almost buckled Lucille's knees. She leaned on the counter for support and fought for control. She hadn't fainted when five-year-old Jackie tried to fly off the roof. She wouldn't now. She concentrated on breathing. With a degree of calmness came clarity: She had to find a weapon.

A knife. Restaurants always have sharp knives. None on or under the counter. None with the silverware. Maybe near the desserts. "I haven't had anything but an apple since lunch. Do you mind if I have a piece of cake and a cup of coffee?"

The gunman glanced at the elderly couple. They'd eaten half their cake. "Why not? And get me a piece."

Lucille gave him the last piece of cake and took a piece of apple pie for herself. No knife anywhere in sight. What else could she use as a weapon?

Restaurants battle bugs. A squirt from a can of insect spray could blind him at a crucial moment. She saw no spray cans, but a big can of cleanser sat by her feet. Cleansers are poison. If she could talk him into a hamburger, she could knead in some cleanser.

He stuffed half his cake in his mouth.

So he was hungry. "Would you mind if I make myself a hamburger? I could make one for you, too."

"I didn't come here to eat! You stay right there where I can see your hands."

She took a bite of pie and searched the countertop for anything heavy enough to hit him with. Nothing but little plastic bowls half full of sugar packets.

She had only her experience to use against him. "I'd get out of here, out of Maryland, if I were you. You shot a deputy sheriff. The sheriff's department is going to come looking for him, and then they're coming after you."

He shifted in his seat. "They don't know to look here, and they won't notice his car in that dark lot. I sure as hell didn't."

A car pulled into the parking lot, swung around, and drove back out again.

The gunman slammed his fist down on the counter. "Damn it, damn it, damn it! He'll kill me if I don't pay him tonight."

9:30. Desperation brought inspiration. "Drive me to an ATM, and I'll get the money for you."

"Real big of you. I know you really care whether I get killed." He shook the gun, now in his left hand, at her. "You figure the others will call the cops, and they'll be watching for me."

"It's your call."

He jiggled on the stool. "I don't like doing this, you know. It's not my style. I got no choice."

Lucille tried to look sympathetic. "I can see that you're desperate." Could he see that she was?

A telephone rang, and the gunman sprang up. "Where's the damn thing at?"

Ronda raised her head. "Under the counter, this side of the cash register."

"Let it ring." He stepped in front of Lucille.

She put her palms flat on the counter. If she could knock the receiver off the hook when he sat down, she could say something to let the operator know what was going on. She slapped herself mentally. What operator? Computers operated the phones these days. Still . . . She counted nine rings.

When the ringing stopped, the gunman pulled the connecting wire out of the receiver. Holding a finger to his lips, he tiptoed to the kitchen door with a gun in his left hand. He opened it a crack and then a little more. "He's still out. What time is it?"

"9:35." Jackie would be here in ten minutes.

He walked back to the stool. "Too late to go anyplace else now."

Lucille's heart pounded. She had to do something. "This coffee's old and cold. Mind if I fix a fresh pot?"

He studied her. "Okay. No funny stuff."

Fingers trembling, she removed the used coffee packet and put in a fresh one. Careful not to hurry, she emptied and refilled the pot and poured the water into the coffee machine. Turning back to the counter, she glanced at the couple.

The woman's lips moved and her hands were folded as though in prayer, but she was staring at Lucille like a cat watching a mouse hole.

"Would you like fresh coffee, too?" What had the man done with his cane? It had been leaning on the table when she carried the coffee to them.

"A fresh cup would be nice," the woman said.

Lucille took three clean mugs from the shelf and lined them up on the counter as close to the gunman as she dared. 9:39. Jackie would be here in five to ten minutes.

Three minutes later, the coffee stopped running into the pot. She picked it up and filled the mugs to the brim. Leaving the pot on the counter, she carried two cups to the booth. "Careful. It's really hot."

The older woman nodded. "I understand."

Did she? Lucille strolled back behind the counter and picked up her mug with her left hand. A car turned into the lot and pulled up by the door. Jackie.

"Finally," the gunman said, pulling up his hood to hide his ski mask and sticking his hands into his sweatshirt pockets. "Not a word from nobody."

Jackie sat in the car a full minute before getting out. She ran the few feet to the front door and pulled it open. "What are you doing behind the counter?"

Lucille flung her coffee at the gunman.

He ducked and raised his right hand to protect his face, but the coffee drenched his mask. "God damn it!" He pulled a gun out of his sweatshirt pocket with his left hand.

She threw the pot at him.

The old man swung his cane down on the gun, knocking it to the floor.

Jackie had drawn her gun. "Hands on your head, sir."

He complied. "Damn it! Damn it! Damn it!"

"Mom, what's going on?"

"He's got a gun in his right pocket," Lucille warned, relieved that her voice didn't quiver. "We need an ambulance."

The white-haired woman reached into her purse. "I'll call 911."

"Cut me loose," Corporal Picatti called from the kitchen.

Lucille rushed in, grabbed a knife from an array on the wall, and sawed at the tape. "Are you badly hurt?"

"I got one hell of a headache, but I can make the arrest."

The rounds of tape finally gave way.

Tape dangling from each wrist, he pushed himself into a sitting position. He brushed dried blood from his right eye before gripping the table to pull himself up.

Lucille's knees gave way as Picatti staggered through the door. She eased down on the floor and put her head between her knees to clear it. When the whirling stopped, she struggled to her feet and hurried into the dining room to watch her daughter the policewoman at work.

The gunman sprawled face down over the counter with his legs spread and his wrists handcuffed behind his back.

Corporal Picatti ripped off the coffee-soaked ski mask to reveal a blotchy, paper-white face and a mop of greasy, brown hair.

Lucille guessed him to be seventeen.

The deputy sighed. "I thought I recognized the voice. You won't get out of this one by going to drug rehab." He stepped back and grinned at Jackie. "If you're as cool under fire as your mother, you're going to be a great police officer."

Jackie laughed. "Awesome, isn't she? The only thing that scares Mom is crossing the Chesapeake Bay Bridge."

Carolyn Mulford has recently moved from nonfiction to fiction and from Silver Spring, Maryland, to Columbia, Missouri. Her first book-length fiction, *The Feedsack Dress,* was published by Cave Hollow Press in July 2007. She is working on a traditional mystery series in which a knowledge of genealogy helps solve murders and an edgier series in which a former CIA covert operative guns for murderers in rural Missouri. A former magazine editor, Carolyn's nonfiction includes a travel book, a biography of Elizabeth Dole, international conference reports, magazine articles for general and special audiences, and newsletters for corporate communicators.

THE TIDE ALSO RISES

by Jayne Ormerod

It started with a splash and ended with a bang. The type of bang you never want to hear when looking up the nostrils of a pistol. Nor something you expect to hear when giving 1,000 pea-sized oysters their bi-weekly bath.

"Noisy buggers, ain't they?" Mrs. McAllister's too-much-whiskey-and-cigarettes voice startled me. I thought I was alone in my bungling efforts to haul what seemed like twelve miles of green hose from the house, across two acres of lawn, and down the high-above-the-marsh-grass dock. When I looked up, I saw the Mrs. Kravitz of Beacon's Creek staring at me from her Adirondack chair. Her beady eyes made me feel guilty. For what, I hadn't a clue.

"Huh?" I grunted. I hated it when my students "huh"-ed me, but the 102-degree heat combined with physical efforts of a body trained in more leisurely pursuits — like lounging in the hammock while losing myself in a sizzling romance — had made me grumpy. And I resented being watched. True south-ern manners required an offer of assistance. I now understood what Cherise had meant when she'd whispered to me, *Watch out for Mrs. McAllister. She's a Yank.*

"The egrets," Mrs. McAlister said, nodding in the direc-tion of a large, white, dangly legged bird soaring over head. "Noisy buggers."

The shore birds screeched in a way that sounded like a woman being strangled. "Oh, yeah. Took some getting used to." I continued my heaving and hoing of the hose. I needed at least ten more feet to reach the end of the dock, but the rubber tube wouldn't budge. I thought I'd got the best end of the deal when my friend had offered me two months rent-free at her recently inherited, *Coastal Living*-inspired home overlooking the marshes of Beacon's Creek and the Chesapeake Bay beyond, in exchange for caring for the oysters. Right now, I was thinking I'd been hoodwinked. Some things look better on paper.

The foster oyster program is part of the Save the Chesa-peake Bay project. The "Tschiswapeki," as the Native Ameri-cans called it, meant "Great Shellfish Bay." But 20th-century over-harvesting, disease, and pollution has reduced the popu-lation by more than ninety-nine percent. With each oyster fil-tering fifty gallons of water per day and their numbers so greatly reduced, it didn't take a nuclear physicist to figure out the bay was in need of life support.

Part of the solution is repopulating the oysters. People like my friend Cherise do their part by raising pea-sized infants to baseball-sized adolescence in a mesh bag settled in a large PVC pipe-and-wire nest floating off the end of their pier. After a year of care, the oysters are loaded onto a skiff and sent out to the bay. With a ceremonious splash, they're dumped over-board to start a new oyster reef. The little shellfish get busy fil-tering, and the bay's health improves. Marginally. It's a very small piece in a very large, problematic puzzle.

Cherise was to be commended for her role in it. Only she had bailed for a summer course in petit fours at the Cordon Bleu. This enabled me to fulfill my lifelong dream of a summer spent along the shore. My only responsibilities were the bi-weekly rinsing of mud off the mesh bag, and plucking out fiddler crabs that had bellied up to an all-you-can-eat oyster buffet. Like I said, some things look better on paper.

I used the hem of my T-shirt to wipe my brow and lips. Experienced hose wrangler I'm not, but common sense told me it must have snagged on something. I didn't relish the idea of the long trek back to the house, especially in the three-inch strappy sandals that had looked like perfect by-the-sea attire when I'd spotted them in the store window. I sighed and did what any blue-blooded southern girl who didn't want to sweat would do — I grabbed the hose tight and yanked for all I was worth.

The hose unengaged. I stumbled backward. My heel caught between two boards. I fell with a splash into Beacon's Creek. It being low tide and all, it was more Beacon's Mud Flats, and I ended up with mud in places a lady doesn't discuss in polite company.

And to make my embarrassment complete, Mrs. McAllister was laughing her ass off.

I wanted to scream. And then I did, when I realized that what I thought was a stick tangled in my hair was really the hand of a dead man.

▅ ▅ ▅

Shock is a funny thing. Despite the sizzling temperature, I shivered like a pair of cheesy wind-up teeth under Mrs. McAlister's tattered quilt. It wasn't so much the sucking sound of the mud wanting to keep its treasure as the police had pulled the body from the water. Nor the front row seat as they stretched the bloated, lifeless, crab-picked body on the dock. Not even wiping off the mud from the victim's face and proclaiming, "It's Elliott King," before covering him with a tarp. No, my shock had its roots in the repetitive and accusatory tone of the detective's questions. And I didn't find his crooked hat imprinted with "Guilty Until Proven Innocent" the least bit amusing. Granted, he'd been called in from a fishing trip with his son and hadn't had time to change clothes, but how hard would it have been to switch into his professional ball cap?

"Do you need anything?" asked the freckle-faced young cop assigned to making sure I didn't run screaming for the hills.

"Yeah. A glass of pinot noir would be great. Second shelf in the fridge." I looked at him and he looked at me — that same *Youdidit* stare that I'd suffered under too often today. "On second thought, make it a double."

"There's a program for that," he said to me, sliding his hands along his utility belt until his right one settled on the butt of his gun. "Called AA. They meet every Thursday in the basement of the First Presby —"

"I'm not an alcoholic, you idiot." The fact that I insulted one of Beacon's Creek finest was proof that I wasn't in my right mind. I took a deep breath.

"That's not what Mz. McAlister told us."

"What does that crazy old busybody know? I've never said more than a dozen words to her." Not civil words, anyway. The ones that had spewed from the darkest recesses of my mind when I'd found that body and she'd taken her sweet time calling 911 didn't count.

"Mz. McAlister makes it her business to know everything that's going on along the creek."

"Sounds like somebody should remind Mrs. McAlister that curiosity killed the cat. Now how about that wine?"

"You can't drink away —"

"Listen. I'm covered in mud and smell like dead fish. I've shark rolled with a dead man, and donated my brand new shoes to the bay. Now I need a small glass of wine." The officer stared at me. "Now!" I used my sternest teacher voice, which garnered the required action. He'd probably get busted to meter maid when his sergeant found out he was playing wine steward, but my nerves were wound like a Slinky and needed some serious un-kinking.

He returned minutes later with an iced-tea glass filled to the brim with ruby red liquid. I settled back in the hammock and took a long sip. Well, *Webster's* would probably define it a gulp. My gaze skipped over the disapproving eyes of the officer and out over the marsh. "You say he's a local boy?" I asked.

"Yessum. Scotty King's eldest. Moved to Hot-lanta about three months ago. His momma held a big shindig in the basement of the First Presbyterian Church the night 'fore he left. Must a' been over a hundred people there. Real nice party. Catered 'n everything." Officer O'Grady smacked his lips as if he'd just finished gnawing on a turkey leg.

"Any guess as to how he died?" I took another gulp, then swirled the glass and watched the wine ebb and flow. A small amount dribbled over the rim, and I licked it the way I would have a melting ice cream cone.

"I'm not a forensics expert, but I'd say the bullet through his heart's probly what done him in."

The gurney laden with a tarp-covered body rolled within five feet of where I sat. That image, the sounds of the creaky conveyance, the smell of brackish water and rotting flesh, would haunt my dreams for the rest of my life.

⌐ ⌐ ⌐

Funerals are funny things. At least Mrs. McAlister seemed to think so. She sat next to me, snorting and guffawing like we were front and center at a comedy club. Granted, Reverend Hanna's overly dramatic reading of "Crossing the Bar" was worthy of an eye roll, but not side-splitting hysterics. I gave her a sharp elbow in the ribs. "Hush, now," I hissed through clenched teeth.

"Oh, hush yourself," she said in what we in the teaching world call an outside voice. And she sure could throw a mean elbow for such a feeble-looking seasoned citizen.

I massaged my side and slunk lower in my seat, trying to ignore the disapproving glares of those around us. I regretted accepting my nosy neighbor's invitation to accompany her to the funeral. She'd said it would be therapeutic and put an end to my nightmares. I was beginning to think spending the afternoon in her company might spark worse ones. "I don't see what's the least bit funny about Elliott's death," I hissed back.

She leaned in close, her raspy words tickling my ear. "It's not his death that I'm laughing at, but the hypocrites sitting here pretending they care he's gone. I guarantee you more than half are here because they think the killer is among the ranks and they want to be able to brag they rubbed elbows with a murderer." Her gaze darted around the room then back at me. "And I know for a fact everyone is here for the fried chicken dinner that follows the service. Elliott's Memaw hired The Gravy Train to cater." Mrs. McAlister settled back. A Mona Lisa-like smile worked its way across her wrinkled, weathered skin. She'd probably been quite a looker in her youth, what with those high cheekbones and perky nose, but the years had not been kind to her.

I thought about what she'd said, and my scalp felt like somebody was rolling a piecrust crimper from the base of my skull all the way over the top of my head. Could the killer really be among us?

🔫 🔫 🔫

"It takes three things to prove murder in a court of law." Mrs. McAlister continued her short course in Murder Investigation 101.

But my mind wasn't on the murder. It was on licking the chicken grease from my fingers. To. Die. For. And the pineapple coleslaw? Words can not express the gastronomic pleasure. I shoveled another forkful into my not-quite-empty mouth. Three more bites and I'd be an official member of the clean-plate club, with just enough room left in my stomach for a generous helping of warm peach cobbler. Mmm mmm mmm.

"Way I see it, you have means and opportunity, but I'm having trouble with the motive."

I choked.

Mrs. McAlister smacked me on the back so hard I hocked up food I'd eaten two days ago. I sputtered and coughed and wheezed and gasped. Finally I managed a coherent defense. "Me?"

"The police chief told me just this morning that Elliott'd been lying in the mud for two weeks."

"So?"

"You've been living at the Montague place for two weeks."

"So?"

"Body found at the end of your dock."

"So?"

"I've seen you out on the dock."

"So?"

"You have experience with guns."

I felt the blood drain from my face. "How . . . "

Mona Lisa smiled again before speaking. "Cherise bragged on you. Wanna tell me about it?"

"Nope." My gaze dropped to my plate of food, and I pushed it away. My taste for peach cobbler was replaced by a churning of gruesome memories. Blood. Intestines. The smell of death. A terrible, horrific incident our senior year in high school. Cherise and I had both been dumped by our boyfriends and drowned our sorrows in mango margaritas. Getting tattoos seemed like the greatest idea in the world. While we stumbled along the sleazy side of town in search of a tattoo parlor, a young kid jumped us from behind and held a gun to Cherise's head. She kicked him where it counts and he dropped the gun. I grabbed it. He pulled a knife. I pulled the trigger. The way

Cherise tells it, I saved her life. From my perspective, I killed another human being.

Fighting the bile gurgling just beneath my tonsils, I excused myself and went to the ladies' room. Cold water to my wrists and cheeks calmed me a bit, but my legs still felt like wet noodles. I collapsed onto the green velveteen chaise longue and allowed myself a moment of self-pity. Mrs. McAlister seemed hell bent on pinning Elliott's murder on me. The only question was, why?

🔫 🔫 🔫

Dusk had settled into a magnetic blue by the time I emerged from the First Presbyterian Church out to the parking lot. No sign of Mrs. McAlister's ghost-gray Beemer. That suited me just fine, because I really didn't want to ride in a car with someone who thought I had the ability to kill another human being.

Cherise's house was three miles outside of town, down a sparsely populated road. My feet had protested when I'd squeezed them into the two-sizes-too-small, three-inch heels (that had been too cute and too price-reduced to pass up), and they weren't at all happy with the prospect of walking that far. The nearest taxi cab was over 30 miles away. I weighed my options: Call Mrs. McAlister and beg her to come get me; hitch a ride with a stranger; or take my shoes off and hoof it to my temporary digs. It was such a beautiful night, I chose option C, and headed south along the sand- and sea-oats-lined road.

My time in the ladies room had proved fruitful. I'd overheard enough conversations to understand the number one suspect in Elliott's murder was not me, thankfully, but a guy by the name of Scary Jerry. Associated with drugs, gambling, and prostitution in the area, he was not exactly a pillar of the community. Current conjecture was Elliott had tried to nose in on Scary Jerry's turf. Elliott's relocation to Atlanta was to be a fresh start for him. So how had he ended back in Beacon's Creek? And dead, at that?

Scary Jerry had motive, and I'm guessing means, since carrying a gun was probably a job requirement in his line of work. All that was left was opportunity. I allowed myself a Walter

Mitty-type fantasy of solving the murder myself. Concluding, of course, with a nose thumbing at my neighbor when I accepted an honorarium from the police chief.

The sound of a diesel engine jarred me from my thoughts. Headlights swept across my path, and I stepped off the road to wait for it to pass. Instead, a red pick-em-up truck slowed down and pulled off the road, the tires rolling within inches of my toes.

"Need a lift, little lady?"

I looked at the driver illuminated by the orange glow of the dashboard lights. Dark suit. Curly graying hair. Crooked smile. Dumbo ears. I remembered him from the funeral, so he wasn't a complete stranger. I knew better than to accept rides from strangers. More importantly, he reminded me of Andy Griffith, the sheriff who never carried a gun. He seemed harmless, and I've always been a good judge of character.

"That would be great." I opened the door and tossed my shoes on the vinyl seat before climbing in myself. "I should probably trade in my stilettos for flip flops if I'm going to be hiking around here." I slammed the truck door behind me and relaxed against the seat. My feet felt happier already.

Too much gas without sufficient release of the clutch had the engine roaring and the gravel spinning. I grabbed the "Oh Shit" handle over my head and held on for all I was worth.

"You're McAlister's new neighbor, ain'tchye?"

It occurred to me my driver's speech was slurred. And he was having trouble staying between the lines on the road.

"Name's Jerry."

As in Scary Jerry? My stomach dropped as if an elevator had just plummeted seventy-five stories. Jerry's a common enough name, I reminded myself. There had to be more than one in town. "Nice to meet you." My voice sounded light and, I hoped, carefree. Two summers at drama camp were paying off. "I'm house sitting for my friend Cherise. She's in France. In cooking school. Something she's wanted to do since she was a little girl." In this small town, I suspected he knew that already, but I always babble to cover my nervousness. And riding shotgun with a drunk driver who might — or might not, I hoped —

be a killer made me more nervous than I had ever been in my life.

We cruised through a stop sign while driving on the wrong side of the road. I slipped my hand down and wrapped it around the cool metal of the door handle. At the first sign of speeds below 20 mph, I planned to roll out. I figured my odds of survival were better out of the truck than in.

"Nice place Cherise got up 'chere. What luck her uncle kicked the bucket. But he had a bit a help, if you know what ah mean."

No, I didn't know what he meant at all. Cherise hadn't said much about her uncle's *modus moriendi*.

I had a super sick feeling in the pit of my stomach. And it wasn't from bad chicken or swervy driving. "Umm . . . " I cleared the gravel from my throat. "What makes you think it wasn't an accident?" It occurred to me I didn't really want to know the answer, because people who have knowledge of how others were murdered often ended up dead themselves.

"Just say, it's for Witchy McAlister ta know 'n' for you ta find out."

The truck skittered to a stop, taking Cherise's mailbox with it. I banged open the door and slipped to safety. "Thanks," I called to the taillights fading into the darkness and the illuminated license plate that said SCRYJRY. "I think," I muttered up to the star-filled sky.

▄▀ ▄▀ ▄▀

Armed with a goblet of Beaujolais, I began a search for anything I could learn about Cherise's Uncle Henry's death. I had a feeling his and Elliott's untimely demises were intricately entwined. And a suspicion Scary Jerry was the missing link.

An Internet search provided me the basics. Henry Wilson Montague had made his millions in plastics. While reaching the pinnacle of financial success, Henry's life was a lesson in money not being able to buy happiness. He married young, but his wife died giving birth to their only child, Lilibeth, who died in a tragic accident at the age of seventeen. Despite further investigation, I couldn't find anything about the circumstances of her death.

Henry had retired one month before his death, settling into the coastal retreat I now occupied. He'd purchased the place on a whim. According to what I found online, he'd suffered a heart attack driving to the grocery store and slammed into a speeding semi truck. No mention of him taking anyone else to heaven with him, thank God.

What did Jerry know that the medical examiner didn't?

A thorough search of rooms, closets, desks, medicine cabinets, and storage bins revealed no trace of Henry's habitation. In the four months Cherise had lived here, she'd successfully de-uncled the place. Not so much as a picture or piece of mail with his name on it.

Sometime after Conan O'Brian had signed off and before the Early Early Morning Show heralded the dawn of a new day, I dragged my tired body up the attic stairs. Eureka. I was met with a sea of cardboard boxes, all labeled "HM's stuff." What I wouldn't have given for some sort of identification or marking that said "Look here for the clue to the murders." The only thing to do was go through them box by box by box. Fortified with two liters of Diet Coke and a sleeve of Fig Newtons, I set to work.

The first thing I learned about Henry Montague was that he was a pack rat. I'd never seen so much junk in my life. Dating way back to his childhood, there were thousands of moldy, mildewy mementoes that set me to sneezing with each opened box.

The second thing I learned was that Henry had not always been honest in his business dealings. Seven boxes of files of legal suits and counter suits accused him of everything from fraud to intellectual property theft. I thought I'd hit pay dirt when I found an entire folder of death threats, but the dates were when Scary Jerry would have been playing with plastic guns.

My head felt like a bowling ball and my shirt sleeve was soaked through with nasal drainage when I came across a red satin journal. It needed to be read. I needed fresh air. Not to mention more caffeine and cookies. So I headed downstairs and out into the sunshine. The heat wave had passed and the morning bordered on cool, at least by southeast Virginia standards. The hammock, stretched between two gloriously green maple trees, called to me. I answered. The ropes cradled me as I fed my hunger and curiosity with equal enthusiasm.

Lilibeth, the Teenage Years did not disappoint. I followed the emotional rollercoaster of Henry's daughter from the age of fifteen (when she defied her father and snuck out to meet a bad boy named Roscoe) through her seventeenth birthday. The drama played out through the very last entry:

> *Daddy gave MY earrings to Miriam. The ones he'd promised would be MINE on my 18th birthday. I want to kill him. And I will. And I'll make Miriam watch and then I'll kill her, too. A slow and painful death. And she'll beg me to stop. And she'll cry and tell me how she never wanted those old earrings anyway, even if they were a gift to my grandma from a crowned prince. She'll try to convince me I have the perfect coloring for emeralds. That I deserve them and she'd never be worthy. Never. I'll laugh and dangle them in her face as she takes her last breath . . .*

Only in Hollywood would the girl have faked her own death and waited 50 years to fulfill her vow to kill her father. Despite hours of searching, I was no closer to unearthing Henry's and Elliot's killer than I had been last night.

Needing something physical to do to keep awake, I decided to give the oysters their overdue bath. I hadn't ventured back onto the pier since the discovery of Elliot's body four days ago. And if I thought about it very long, I'd talk myself out of it again today. I marched to the corner of the garage, grabbed the end of the hose, and dragged it across the yard and down to the dock.

The creek circled and swirled as it ebbed back to sea. Tides run on a twelve-and-a-half-hour cycle, which doesn't match up to a twenty-four-hour world. That means each high and low tide occurs thirty minutes later each day. I wondered where in the tide cycle Elliott's body had been dumped. If it had been me, I'd have tossed at ebb tide, like now, so the body would be carried out to the bay, never to be found. A flood tide would carry it up the creek, where the water became increasingly shallow and the body increasingly likely to be discovered.

Maybe Elliott's body had been tossed into the middle of the bay and the tide had carried it to this dock? Maybe the killer hadn't been a waterman, hadn't known that summer tides aren't as high as winter tides? Maybe the body had been buried in the mud, and only through my clumsiness had been uncovered?

I shrugged off the feeling of a ghost walking across my grave as I looked across the marsh grass. A lone, long-legged egret stood above the shallow water, not moving. Waiting, waiting, waiting for his breakfast to come to him. Fast as lightning, his head jerked beneath the surface and emerged clutching a silver fish. Massive wings spread out, and the bird flew elsewhere to enjoy his feast.

The facts of the murders swirled with the vision of the dangly legged egret and my visualization of Lilibeth's dangly emerald earrings. Faces swam before me: from the funeral, from the newspaper clippings, from Henry's photo albums. I started to add two plus two but no matter how I ciphered, I came up with six.

Soft footsteps scratched along the dock. I turned. Great. The last person I wanted to see. Mrs. McAlister. And I doubly didn't want to see her when I saw what was in her hands. In one, she clutched the cherry-red diary. In the other, a handgun.

My heart stopped beating. My lungs stopped respirating. The only autonomic response working on me right now were my sweat glands. It felt like Niagara Falls rushing under my arms.

"So, you figured it all out?" Her raspy voice had me wanting to clear my throat.

"Huh?"

She wiggled the diary. She waggled the gun.

Then it hit me. At the funeral she'd worn dangly emerald earrings. She was a Yank. Henry's business had been based near Cleveland, Ohio. Miriam McAlister had killed Lilibeth Montague before Lilibeth had killed her. "Why kill Henry after all these years?" The sound of my voice startled me. I hadn't meant to speak my thoughts aloud.

"He retired, found the diary, and read it. Of course, I

denied it when he accused me. He didn't believe me, so he moved here to make what's left of my life a guilty hell."

"And Elliot?"

"Because he'd done my dirty work by slipping some oleander to Henry so he'd have a heart attack and was blackmailing me for more money."

"So you killed Elliott and were trying to frame me." No question. Just a statement of fact.

"Yup. Couldn't believe my luck when you settled in."

Faster than that egret had snagged his breakfast, Mrs. McAlister raised the gun and pulled the trigger. With a bang and a flash, I went to my watery grave, snuggled up next to the baby oysters.

Jayne Ormerod is the original Ghostbuster. Raised in a 200-year-old farmhouse that once served as a brothel, Jayne's imagination had herself and others convinced of the presence of restless spirits. The experiences taught her how to spin a really good story, which was a useless talent in her career as an accountant. She married a Naval officer, and after fifteen moves in conjunction with his career decided she needed a more transportable (and spiritually satisfying) vocation so turned to writing. Jayne measures her success not only in publication, but also by the euphoric feeling at the end of a really good day of writing.

INKED TO DEATH

by Shelley Shearer

Red ink stained her fingers, frosted by sand from burrowing beneath the driftwood. Maya tried to enjoy the scent of fresh sea spray now that the lotion-covered sunbathers had left Cape Henlopen State Park for the season, but guilt shadowed the morning. After five years as Ethan's letterboxing partner and two as his wife, Maya had ventured out on her own for the first time.

Letterboxing had been their primary activity as a couple since her friend Bryn had introduced them to the hobby. Maya's guilt doubled as she remembered giggling like school kids with Ethan the first time they solved the clues and found a box. But lately Ethan had been at work more than he was home. No more weekends of printing off clues and playing treasure hunter as they searched neighborhood parks. Now her weekends consisted of mindless television surfing or joining Bryn in whatever quirky hobby she had taken up.

That Sunday morning, her birthday no less, Ethan went to the office to finalize an audit. So after a few moments of self-pity with a chaser of truffles, Maya grabbed her letterboxing backpack and treated herself to a day out.

She dusted the sand from her hands and wiped the top layer of grime from the plastic storage box. "Letterbox. Please Do Not Destroy" was written in permanent marker across the top to alert anyone who stumbled across it by accident.

▗ ▗ ▗

Her cell phone rang with Ethan's signature tone before she had a chance to pry open the box. "Yes," she answered trying not to sound angry.

"Hi, hon. Look, I know we had reservations tonight, but I'm not going to be able to make it. This audit has to be finished tonight."

Maya mouthed the words as he said them, her knuckles turning white from gripping the phone. She closed her eyes and counted to five before trying to answer. The last few times she'd snapped back with a sarcastic response, he'd used it as an excuse to stay away more.

"We'll do something special this weekend. I promise." Maya heard voices in the background, but she couldn't make out the words. Before she could respond, he hung up.

"No, Ethan, that's okay," she said to the dead phone in her hand. "Really. I understand your work is more important than a silly dinner." Or me for that matter.

Maya threw the phone into her backpack, taking pleasure in the thud when it hit her water bottle. She ripped the lid off the letterbox and turned her attention to her find. Every box was unique, but all of them contained a rubber stamp and a logbook. Finding the box was the hard part. Letterboxers were like pirates, offering cryptic puzzles and codes as clues to their hidden treasures.

Inside the box was a rubber stamp of a small dune buggy. Perfect for the location, it would make a nice addition to her logbook. After years of hunting letterboxes, her log contained images of everything from store-bought doggy stamps to a hand-carved replica of the Taj Mahal.

r r r

Maya examined her own stamp, a carved likeness of a fifties housewife complete with petticoat and pearls. Maybe not the most feminist or forward-thinking image, but being a wife was what she'd always wanted. When they had first married, Ethan praised her culinary skills and applauded her new recipes. Now he ate out, claiming he preferred quick and easy meals. Maya suspected what he really preferred were quick and easy meals with someone else.

She settled in to enjoy browsing the previous entries in the logbook, not minding the damp sand. Ethan tended to rush through this part, annoyed when she wanted to read the notations left in the logbook. Sometimes it was nothing more than the finder's name, but sometimes a fun story was jotted down. Maya smiled, remembering the chuckle they shared when they read a log discussing a nude jogger seen on the trails.

Remembering the good times caused her to doubt her

decision to come out on her own. If she stamped in, it would be the first time their stamps had not been entered together. The page would symbolize the loss of something she held very dear. "No harm done," she said as she rewrapped her stamp.

Determined to convince Ethan to stop working and resume their favorite hobby, Maya started to pack everything back up. She flipped the logbook open to see if anyone else had discovered the box. She froze. Not wanting to believe her eyes, she tried to rationalize the entry. Maybe they had been to so many boxes over the years, she'd forgotten they had discovered this one before. But her stamp image was nowhere to be found. Only two were in the logbook so far. Ethan's purple cartoon sheep was unmistakable. Snuggled up next to it, right where her home diva stamp should be, was a penguin in a bikini. Both had signed in four days ago.

🖋 🖋 🖋

The ring of her phone jarred her from her disturbing thoughts.

"Hey, Maya. What's up?" Bryn asked when she answered.

Maya gripped the logbook in her hands and asked flatly, "Do you know anyone with a penguin stamp?"

"Mmm . . . let me think." Maya could hear Bryn tapping her nails, but didn't interrupt with her normal lighthearted humming of the *Jeopardy* theme. She wanted to be told that the stamp was from a scout troop that Ethan's office had adopted, but a penguin in a bikini? Or maybe there was a rogue letterboxer who stole people's stamps and used them. Anything but what Bryn came back with. "Sarah has one, but I haven't letterboxed in awhile so I can't be sure."

Sarah. The penguin had a name, and it wasn't a boy scout.

"You still there?" Bryn asked.

"Yeah, sorry. I, well I went letterboxing on my own today and saw that stamp."

"That's great!" Bryn said. "I'm glad you took my suggestion and went. Ethan won't mind if you enjoy yourself while he's swamped."

"I'm starting to wonder if he's as busy as he says." Maya's

bitterness was impossible to hide. She told Bryn about the log-book.

"Don't panic. Doesn't he work near there? Maybe he needed a quick break from the desk? I wouldn't worry about. Stamp in. Enjoy yourself! I gotta run, but don't forget about our medieval gardening class tomorrow."

▗ ▗ ▗

A small part of her wasn't convinced, but Bryn's assurances helped her feel lighthearted enough to stamp in and re-hide the box. Maybe it was something as innocent as a lunch break. She spent the better part of the day finding six more letterboxes in various areas of the county and seeing the same two stamps side by side at every one. One could have been innocent. Seven crushed her ability to live in denial.

Maya hugged her knees to her chest as she leaned back against the tree, not caring if she was blocking the trail. The final logbook still lay on her lap, the incriminating page taunting her. The icy pain of betrayal melted to embarrass-ment when she read notes left by others. "Cool stamp. Great meeting you two on the trails. I wish my husband would letterbox with me!" Maya wiped her tears, not caring that the stamping ink she had all over her hands smeared her cheek.

▗ ▗ ▗

For two weeks, she played the role of demure housewife, doling out understanding phrases to Ethan when he called to say he'd be late. She needed all the free time she could manage to find the right ingredient, carve the stamp, and choose the perfect hiding location. If Ethan thought her new forgiving persona was odd, he kept it to himself and enjoyed the free-dom.

"Ethan, hon?" Maya grinned, holding the letterboxing backpack in front of her in the doorway of their bedroom.

"Sorry, pet, there's no way I can make it out on the trails today." He shrugged, checking his reflection in the mirror. "Maybe next week."

"Come on, call in sick or something," she urged. "The clue was posted only this morning, and it says there's an added surprise for the first finder."

He focused his attention on her for a moment before looking at the backpack. "Tempting, but maybe we can still be first by next week. Here, let me put the stuff in the car. If I can get out early, I'll come by and pick you up."

She handed over the bag and air kissed his check. "Great. I'll be at Bryn's most of the day helping set up her new garden. Call on the cell."

Maya watched him from the window as he backed out the driveway, already talking on his cell phone. For one instant, she wanted to run after him and tear the clues from his hand, but the memory of a penguin stopped her. If he wasn't cheating, he would be fine. He was the only one who had those clues.

r r r

Later, while Bryn held her hand in the emergency room, Maya didn't have to fake her tears. Even while she carved the complex image of the sheep being sheared and exposed, she had hoped she was wrong. She was numb as the doctor gently explained that Ethan had been found with a lady wandering confused in the woods. He had died en route to the hospital.

"What happened?" Bryn asked when Maya stayed silent.

"Unfortunately, it looks like they sampled the wrong berries. They both showed cases of severe poisoning."

"How awful," Bryn said, squeezing Maya's hand. "The teacher in our gardening class told us about a case of that just last month."

The conversation buzzed in and out of Maya's mind as she stared silently down at her hands. Tomorrow would be another day. She would carve herself a new personal stamp to use. Something exotic and dangerous. But first she'd have to go and recover the box to keep someone else from stumbling across it. Her spare pair of thick rubber gloves would keep the glass shards she'd embedded in the stamp from piercing her skin, but the over-inked stamp and inkpad would still have to be thoroughly washed.

Belladonna wasn't always fatal, but why tempt fate?

An avid letterboxer with over five hundred finds to date, Shelley Shearer finds it a great way to spend time with her husband and two sons and travel to new and interesting parks. In the mundane world, she works full time in the accounting field, while she pursues her Masters in Library Science degree and works on her full-length letterboxing mystery novel. When she has any free time from that, she reads cozy mysteries and urban fantasy, cross stitches, and loves taking up new hobbies that catch her interest.

TWO SISTERS

by Marcia Talley

The elegant Marlborough Apartments (1700 Eutaw Place), erected in 1904 on the location of the nineteenth-century Popelein mansion, closed in 1970. Claribel and Etta Cone, friends of Matisse, Picasso, and Gertrude and Leo Stein, once housed their collection of twentieth century art there. The Marlborough re-opened in 1977, with rehabilitated living units for the elderly, funded by Federal grants.
— Chesapeake Bay Magazine,
November 1997

Trudy plunked a tea bag into a mug and covered it with boiling water. Holding the string, she plunged the bag up and down in the hot liquid, amusing herself by imagining it was her son's head. True, it was Stephen who had provided her with the laptop computer that was her main connection to the outside world these days, but she wouldn't have needed the laptop in the first place if she were still living in her own home instead of a retirement unit in the Marlborough Apartments. Still scowling, Trudy tossed the teabag into the sink. The laptop was probably a hand-me-down anyway, she grumbled, a reject from that fancy-pants insurance agency Stephen ran out of a glass and steel skyscraper overlooking Baltimore's Inner Harbor.

Trudy shuffled to the bedroom of her apartment and powered up the computer. She waited, quietly sipping her tea, as the Windows logo gave way to a blue screen, then to her desktop theme, a family photograph. It featured Trudy surrounded by three of her grandchildren, taken by Goofy at Disney World last fall. She smiled, remembering, as the landscape framing her grandchildren became populated with the familiar icons labeled My Computer, Explorer and Word-Perfect, and by others she didn't know anything about but Stephen sometimes used. Whenever Mr. Bigshot wasn't too busy to visit, that is.

With some effort, Trudy banished Stephen from her

thoughts. She was expecting an e-mail from home. (Former home, she corrected.) Victoria always wrote late Sunday night; her e-mail was the first thing Trudy looked forward to reading on Monday morning.

Trudy double-clicked the Explorer button that would bring up her Comcast Webpage, access to her e-mail account, and news from her best friend. She watched while the screen filled, not with the display she expected, but with a colorful Webpage associated with the Baltimore Museum of Art.

What on earth?

Trudy clicked the back button as Stephen had instructed, but nothing changed. She remained stuck at www.artbma.org, on a page that shouted in uppercase letters: THE CONE COL-LECTION. What the heck was the Cone Collection? A collection of cones and, if so, what kind? Ice cream cones? Traffic cones? Pine cones? Volcanic cones? Rods and cones of the human eye? How very odd.

She scanned the unfamiliar display looking for a button that would lead to her e-mail, but nothing seemed appropriate, so she clicked "Home." The screen cleared, then slowly re-freshed itself: She was back at the Baltimore Museum of Art.

Trudy was caught in a death loop.

Not that Trudy had anything against art. Oh no. She'd heard that Baltimore, Maryland had many fine museums and as soon as she got settled in, she intended to visit some of them, but at that particular moment, all she wanted was her e-mail. Back home the Second Baptists had told Brother Bill knock-off-your-affair-or-else with Janelle Owens, the Sunday school director, and Victoria had promised Trudy an update. Being kept in limbo about hometown gossip was maddening.

When in doubt, reboot, Stephen always said. Trudy tried rebooting, with equal lack of success. When the monitor came to life, there were those damn cones again, cluttering up her screen. A computer glitch. Hell's bells! She'd have to call Ste-phen after all. Serve him right if he had to come and fix it for her; he hadn't been to visit in weeks.

Trudy reached for the phone, punched in Stephen's num-ber, but got his answering machine. After the beep Trudy swal-lowed her pride and purred into the telephone. "Stephen, this is your mother. If you're there, please pick up." She paused a fraction of a second before continuing. "I think I've got a computer virus. Can you come help me out? Thank you!" she caroled, then slammed the receiver into its cradle.

At least Stephen's daughter, Alison, paid attention to her. Her granddaughter's weekly visits were the highlight of her life. Trudy glared at the screen from the Baltimore Museum of Art that refused to disappear, no matter what she clicked on.

She sighed with exasperation. With Stephen not immediately available, she'd have to go to Plan B.

Trudy padded to her closet, slipped out of her nightgown and into a gray fleece jogging suit. In front of the mirror, she adjusted the backs on the diamond-stud earrings Carlton had given her on their fortieth wedding anniversary, then added a strand of Barbara Bush pearls. Still wearing her slippers, she shuffled next door to the apartment Monty shared with his marmalade cat, Fangdango. Monty often joined Trudy's table in the Marlborough's community dining room, and she seemed to remember him babbling about working with computers.

Monty's door had a brass knocker shaped like an anchor. In celebration of Halloween, he'd decorated the knocker with a witch doll made of straw and patchwork fabric, fastened securely with plaid ribbon and raffia. Trudy grabbed the witch around the waist and rapped smartly. On the other side of the door, she heard applause alternating with *dings* as Vanna (she presumed) turned the letters. Trudy knocked again, Pat Sajak was silenced in mid-sentence, and Monty opened the door wearing khaki pants and a blue Oxford button-down shirt under a brown v-neck sweater. Monty had a prize-winning comb-over that defied the laws of gravity. It began an inch above the nape of his neck and swept upward, a comb-over so elaborate that even Donald Trump's hairdresser would have taken three steps backward and fallen to his knees in awe of it.

"I hate to bother you," Trudy began, still smiling over Monty's remarkable hair-do, "but I'm having a problem with my computer. I'm afraid I've got some sort of virus. Can you take a look?"

Monty grinned broadly, revealing a row of perfectly even,

perfectly white teeth that probably rested comfortably in a glass on his bedside table each night. "Been years since I did any troubleshooting," he said, "but let me see what I can do."

It wasn't until Monty was inside her apartment that Trudy remembered the way he had eyeballed her cleavage at dinner the previous Friday, and that her laptop was inextricably hooked up to printers, modems, powerstrips, and such in the bedroom. She certainly didn't want to give the old man ideas! Trudy backed up against the door frame and pointed her neighbor in the right direction. "In there."

She observed from the hallway while Monty sat down in the swivel chair, adjusted his eyeglasses, leaned forward, and peered at her monitor. A few clicks of the mouse later he announced, "You don't have a virus, Trudy, you just changed where 'home' is. See . . . " He flapped a hand, motioning her into the room. Trudy approached cautiously, until she was squinting at the screen over his shoulder. Monty pointed to an icon shaped like a house on the menu bar of her Explorer page. "From what you told me, 'home' should be set to Comcast.net. Look, you have it set for www.artbma.org."

Trudy stared in disbelief. "I didn't change anything, Monty. When it comes to computers, I'm a complete moron. I turn the computer on. I turn the computer off. I click on the little envelope to read my e-mail. That's all I know how to do."

"Well, these things happen," he said, clearly not buying a word of it. "I'll change it back for you."

Several clicks and a flurry of keystrokes later the BMA's Cone Collection Webpage morphed into the Comcast screen she recognized. "Oh thank you!" Trudy gushed, truly and enormously grateful.

"No problem. Anytime." Monte stood, hitched up his pants and grinned toothily.

"Would you like some tea?" she asked. Trudy wanted to dig immediately into her e-mail, but felt she owed her neighbor a little something for his efforts. "The water's still hot."

"Don't mind if I do."

"That was so strange," Trudy said to Monty over her shoulder as he trailed after her down the hall. "What's the Cone Collection, anyway? Do you know?"

"Everyone knows about . . . " then he paused, blushed. "Sorry. I forgot you're new to Baltimore. Claribel and Etta Cone were spinster sisters who started buying Matisse and Picasso back at the turn of the century, back when they were starving artists. Those two old birds amassed the largest collection of Matisses in the world . . . and right here in the Marlborough Apartments! When Etta died, she left it all to the Baltimore Museum of Art. They've got it over there now, in a special wing."

"Goodness!"

"The Cones were personal friends of Gertrude Stein and Alice B. Toklas, too," he added.

Trudy pressed a hand to her chest. "Gertrude Stein? And Toklas? Were the Cone sisters . . . ?" She took a deep breath.

Monty raised an eyebrow, then helpfully filled in the blank. "Lesbians?" He shook his head so vigorously that his comb-over started sliding down the back of his skull like an oversized cinnamon bun. "Hard to say. I've got a book about them somewhere. Be happy to loan it to you."

"Thank you, Monty," she said, warming to her neighbor. "Why don't you go look for it while I put the kettle back on."

Within five minutes, Monty was back. With the book tucked under his arm, he drifted toward the kitchen table, which Trudy had set for tea: a teapot under a rooster-shaped tea cozy, two colorful mugs, her best sterling silver spoons, milk and sugar, and a plate of Milano cookies.

While Monty stirred two heaping spoonfuls of sugar into his tea, Trudy leafed through the pages of the book, *Dr. Claribel and Miss Etta.*

"I see what you mean about the Marlborough Apartments," Trudy said, turning a page. "Oh my goodness! It says here that Etta lived in Eight A. That's my apartment!"

Monty nodded. "And Claribel lived in Eight B. The living and dining room of Claribel's apartment is now my studio."

Trudy ran her fingers gently over a glossy plate of *Woman in Turban.* "It must have been marvelous to see." She sighed wistfully. "All those glorious paintings! And right where we're living, too."

Monty held up a finger. "Hold that thought! Let's go back to the computer."

"What for?" Trudy squinted suspiciously at his departing back, but she was curious, so she set her mug on the table next to Monty's abandoned one, grabbed the book, and followed.

At the end of the hallway Monty turned, stepped aside, and allowed Trudy to enter the bedroom ahead of him. "I just remembered something about the BMA Webpage," he told her. "They've got a virtual tour of the Cones' apartments with all the artwork in place, just as it was when they lived here." He pulled out her chair. "Here. Sit." He pushed the mouse toward Trudy's hand.

Trudy sat, and following Monty's instructions, guided the cursor across the screen to a door, clicked, and watched as it slowly opened to reveal a bedroom stacked high with old-fashioned trunks; paintings covered the walls. She clicked on a painted chest, and a drawer slid open revealing beautiful lace collars and fabric samples. "Oh, my."

"What's over there?" Monty touched the screen with a long finger.

Obligingly, Trudy clicked on another door and found herself floating like a disembodied spirit down a long, narrow corridor lined with paintings. At the end of the corridor, she clicked on another door that swung open to reveal a dining room. To her surprise, a man sporting a trim beard and mustache stood there, one hand thrust casually into the pocket of his three-piece, double-breasted suit, the other resting lightly on a buffet. Trudy stared at the screen. "Who the heck is that?" The image stared back at her through round, black-framed eyeglasses.

Monty snorted. "Looks like Sigmund Freud."

"Don't be silly. What would Sigmund Freud be doing in Etta Cone's dining room?" Trudy reached for Monty's book and flipped to the index, then thumbed through the volume to the page she wanted. "Just as I thought. It's Henri Matisse." She smiled, comparing the photograph in the book with the image on her computer monitor. "He doesn't look much like an artist, does he?"

"It says here that Matisse came to visit Etta in Baltimore

on . . . " Monty squinted through a pair of half glasses at the page Trudy had pointed out to him. ". . . on December 17 and 18, 1930." He glanced up at Trudy and winked. "Spent the night, too. I guess that lays to rest your lesbian theory!"

Trudy scowled at Monty's joke, then continued to cruise around the virtual apartment, examining the paintings. "My gosh!" she exclaimed as she opened a door and found herself (virtually, at least) in a bathroom. "Etta's got oil paintings hanging in the john!"

Monty stole a glance at his watch. "Speaking of johns, I've got to . . . " He winked broadly, ". . . freshen up. Bridge game downstairs in ten. You play?" His eyebrows shot up in anticipation.

"No, but thanks."

"Well, if you have any more trouble getting to your e-mail, you just call me, hear?" He flashed a crooked grin and hurried away.

Trudy washed and put away the tea dishes, then returned to the computer to check on the e-mail she'd neglected. She clicked around the screen the way Monty had shown her, but no matter what she did, she could only return to the Baltimore Museum of Art Webpage and the virtual tour of the Marlborough Apartments. She sat back in her chair. Perhaps she didn't have a virus at all. Maybe her computer was haunted. Maybe she needed an exorcist. Trudy hated to bother Monty again, but if she telephoned her son, he'd think she was a senile old bag. She turned the computer off at the power strip, counted to ten, then turned it back on.

This time, when the monitor came to life, Henri Matisse was standing in a sitting room of some kind, between a piano and an old-fashioned radio. Over the radio hung a portrait of a woman in a yellow dress, seated before an open window. Trudy lingered over the portrait, imagining how it would look hanging on the wall of *her* sitting room, noting with satisfaction how the vibrant colors — the yellow of the woman's dress, the red of the tiles — matched the fabric on her sofa. Then the rumbling of her stomach reminded her that half a Milano cookie hardly constituted a meal and she'd better put on some proper shoes and get downstairs to the dining room.

After lunch — a particularly satisfying grilled tuna and cheese — Trudy kept her appointment with the hairdresser, then hurried back upstairs to her computer. When she logged on this time, Matisse had moved into a hallway, his head partially blocking Trudy's view of a wonderful painting of a dog asleep beneath a table. She clicked her mouse on the painting: *Interior with Dog*. Everything about the painting made her smile: the magnolia branches springing from the blue and white Chinese vase, the colorful wall hanging, the dog's checkered blanket. It burst with life!

Over the course of the afternoon, with each click of her mouse, Trudy found herself falling in love with the paintings that had once, long ago, hung on her walls: *Standing Odalisque Reflected in a Mirror* — a little plump around the middle to be wearing pantaloons and going topless, Trudy thought, but who am I to talk about plump? The exquisite *Anemones and Chinese Vase*, and, her favorite of all, *Interior with Flowers and Parakeets*. She felt like she could reach right into the painting, feel the texture of the embroidered curtain, drink from the tea cup, talk nonsense to the lime-green parakeets. Trudy decided that the next time her granddaughter came to visit, they'd go to the Baltimore Museum of Art and see the paintings in person.

The next morning, all thought of e-mail abandoned, Trudy discovered that Matisse had wandered into a room crammed with dressers and tables. Picasso's famous portrait of Gertrude Stein dominated the room, but it was the smaller portraits flanking the author that interested Trudy the most: charcoal drawings of Etta and Claribel Cone. She zoomed in for a closer examination.

Suddenly, the cursor took on a life of its own, flitting around the screen like a ouiji board, taking Trudy into another room and depositing her in front of a portrait of two women sitting on a balcony, watching a parade. She clicked on the painting and a label popped up: *Festival of Flowers*. Two women. Etta and Claribel?

Trudy stared at the winking cursor, thinking hard. Was Henri Matisse reaching back through time, trying to tell her something? Claribel Cone, she remembered, had died some twenty years before her sister. Maybe she'd been murdered!

Trudy laughed out loud. Better not mention *that* hypothesis to Stephen. She imagined his patronizing smile, his sarcastic, "You've been reading too many mystery magazines, Mother."

To test her theory, Trudy once again referred to the book Monty had given her. No, she read, Claribel had died of pneumonia in 1929 while living in Lausanne, Switzerland. How about Etta, then? She flipped pages until she reached the end of the book. It told her that Etta died of heart failure in 1949. Nothing unusual about that. The old girl must have been almost eighty.

Trudy's tired eyes returned to her monitor where Matisse stared out at her, unblinking. "Henri," she told his image, "you are beginning to creep me out." Maybe she needed a break.

When Trudy returned to her computer following the Tuesday night after-dinner Oldies But Goodies Songfest, Henri Matisse had migrated to another sitting room. Behind Monsieur Matisse, outside his window, it was fall, the leaves on the trees a palate of reds, golds, and greens.

Trudy nearly fell out of her chair. "Holy cow!" she exclaimed aloud. "I recognize that view! That's the window in *my* living room!" Index finger furiously working her mouse, Trudy zoomed in to study the drawings and paintings to the right and left of the artist — a vase of peonies, a landscape by Cezanne. Still, whatever message Matisse was trying to send remained elusive. She adjusted the cushion at the small of her back and leaned into it, thinking. Except for the view of the trees, everything had changed about Etta Cone's apartment over the course of fifty years and two major renovations. Nothing remained on the walls except, except . . . Trudy took a deep, steadying breath. Everything, that is, except the paneling!

Trudy dashed to the kitchen and scrabbled through a drawer, looking for her sturdiest carving knife. Without even pausing to close the drawer, she scurried back to the living room where she sat cross-legged on the floor in front of the window, and began digging at the edges of the paneling. She forced the blade between the paneling and the window sill, twisted the handle. With a screech of nails, the paneling began to separate from the wall. When the opening was large enough, Trudy peeked inside. Nothing but a narrow, dark space. Cautiously, she stuck her hand into the opening and, holding her breath, felt around. A few minutes later, a rusty can of Tab, a handful of nails, two pennies, and a short length of pipe, greasy and dusty with age, littered the floor around her.

Trudy held the pipe to her eye like a telescope. Something was inside. She slid two fingers into the opening and eased out another tube, this one wrapped in oil cloth and tied with two pieces of rough string. With her heart pounding, Trudy carried the tube into her kitchen, untied the strings, and unrolled its contents carefully on the table, weighting the edges down with ceramic teapots from her collection.

She stared, open-mouthed, hardly daring to breathe. On the table before her lay a painting of a woman dressed in oriental robes, lounging in a green and yellow striped armchair. As if the red tile floor hadn't been a dead giveaway, she recognized the chair — Matisse had featured it in *Seated Odalisque, Left Leg Bent*. And the delicate lace curtains in the window were from another painting, *Nude with Spanish Comb*. The artist was unmistakably Henry Matisse. If that wasn't enough to take Trudy's breath away, it was the subject of the portrait that also made her gasp: Etta Cone.

Trudy leaned back against her stove, reeling. A genuine Matisse! With her index finger, she caressed a corner of the lost masterpiece. It must be worth millions! She could sell it, buy a house in the south of France, hire round-the-clock help — now that was assisted living! — and thumb her nose at her stuffy, good-for-nothing son.

But, how on earth had the painting gotten inside the wall? Trudy remembered reading that after Etta died, security guards had been posted at the door while the collection was inventoried prior to moving it to the BMA. Perhaps one of the workers had planned to steal the painting, stashing it there, hoping to come back for it later? A museum employee? Trudy wondered. One of Etta's own staff?

But no, that couldn't be it. During Claribel and Etta's lifetimes, the collection had been extensively catalogued. There were account books, inventories, customs declarations.

Just to be sure, Trudy pored over the Cone inventory in Monty's book, reading it over several times. Nothing remotely resembling this masterpiece was listed among the hundred and forty-nine paintings, ninety-seven drawings, fifty-four sculptures, one hundred and fourteen prints, and three illustrated books that had been among the sisters' Matisse collection at the time of Etta's death.

As far as Trudy was concerned, there could be only one explanation: Matisse must have brought the painting with him when he visited Baltimore in 1930. It had been a gift for Etta, one she'd not wanted to share. Trudy knew with absolute certainty that Etta herself had hidden it.

For the next few days, Trudy did little else but worry about what to do with the painting. Rather than join the other residents for dinner, she ate yogurt topped with Raisin Bran alone in her apartment. Monty knocked on her door several times; the social director called to check on her, too, but she'd sent them both away, pleading a migraine.

Not that she was lying, exactly. Henri Matisse had turned into a major headache. Every time she went for her e-mail, he'd materialize over her inbox, standing by the virtual front door to Apartment 8-D. And, was it her imagination, or did he appear to be frowning?

In self-defense, Trudy would shut off the computer, watching as Matisse's image faded away. But morning after morning, when she powered up, the artist would be back, loitering by the front door. She figured he'd stand there forever unless she did what she had to do.

Trudy picked up the phone and punched the buttons. "Alison, sweetie," she purred when her granddaughter answered, "How would you like to visit the art museum?"

r r r

Before long, Trudy's e-mail returned to normal: no-cost mortgages, cheap Canadian prescriptions, offers of untold wealth from exiled Nigerian princes, and miracle concoctions guaranteed to enlarge body parts she didn't possess, but perhaps the Nigerian princes did. Sam's Club wanted her to renew her membership, and Victoria was annoyed that she hadn't stayed in touch. Brother Bill had ditched Janelle, Victoria announced triumphantly, but his wife had kicked him out of the house anyway.

In the virtual world on the other side of her computer screen, Matisse would show up in the dining room from time to time, but for the most part, he was gone, back to Nice, Trudy supposed. She almost missed him.

But week in and week out, Alison, her reliable (and clever!) granddaughter would meet her at Gertrude's (ten percent discount to BMA members!) where they would lunch on crab cakes, and visit Etta Cone, hanging happily on the north wall in the Cone Collection, next to her favorite painting, *Interior with Flowers and Parakeets*.

Lunch was Trudy's treat. It was Alison, after all, who first uttered the magic words — finders keepers; the third-year-law student who said with some authority, "You own the condo, Granny. What's inside its walls belongs to you."

Stephen had sputtered and blustered, of course, but it was Alison who brokered the deal with the Baltimore Museum of Art, resulting in a fat check funded by a National Endowment for the Arts Purchase Grant and a generous gift from the Rory L. and Carol A. Chase Foundation.

Sitting at her computer in recent days, Trudy enjoyed pulling her bank account balance up on the screen, tracing her finger over all the numbers to the left of the decimal point. A cottage in the South of France — near Nice? — was not entirely out of the question.

"We'll case the joint, Granny," Alison had laughed the day they logged on to www.cunard.com to see about booking passage on the Queen Mary 2.

Trudy guided her cursor over the screen and clicked "Book Now." "Assisted living at its finest, my dear."

She was certain both Henri and Etta would approve.

Marcia Talley is the Agatha and Anthony Award-winning author of *Dead Man Dancing* and six previous Hannah Ives mysteries, all set in Maryland. She is author/editor of two star-studded collaborative serial novels, *Naked Came the Phoenix* and *I'd Kill For That* set in a fashionable health spa and an exclusive gated community, respectively. Her short stories appear in more than a dozen collections including "With Love, Marjorie Ann" and "Safety First", both Agatha award nominees, and the multi-award-winning "Too Many Cooks", a humorous retelling of Shakespeare's Macbeth from the viewpoint of the three witches from *Much Ado About Murder*, edited by Anne Perry. A recent story, "Driven to Distraction" won the Agatha Award, was nominated for an Anthony, and selected for inclusion in *The Deadly Bride And 21 of the Years Best Crime and Mystery Stories*.

Marcia is immediate past president of the Chesapeake Chapter of Sisters in Crime, and serves as secretary for Sisters in Crime National. She is on the board of the Mid-Atlantic Chapter of the Mystery Writers of America. She divides her time between Annapolis, Maryland and living aboard an antique sailboat in the Bahamas.